Black Gold Death in the Sun

A Novel

C E Osbourne

Eloquent Books
New York, New York

Eloquent Books
An imprint of Writers Literary & Publishing Services, Inc.
845 Third Avenue, 6th Floor – 6016
New York, NY 10022
www.eloquentbooks.com

ISBN: 978-1-934925-22-5, 1-934925-22-5

Printed in the United States of America

Cover Illustrations: ©Stephen Coburn,
©Steven Pepple / DreamsTime.com

Book Design: Stacie Tingen

Dedications

This novel is dedicated to three ladies in my life.

My mother Mary Stevens who passed away in October 2006, who brought me up as well as she could in a tough environment and taught me always to finish what I started no matter what the odds.

My friend Penny Cutler who encouraged me to rewrite the book after the original was destroyed. Thank you.

And last but by no means least my partner and soon to be wife Maeve whose love, affection, and support has made my life the joy it is today.

Contents

Foreword

This story is set around 1980 just before the Shah of Iran, "Shah Reza," was ousted from power by the return of Ayatollah Khomeini from France. It is set in a time when Middle Eastern countries were seeing a vast increase in their wealth and were building the infrastructure of the modern Middle East of today.

In that time, the expatriate workforce was made up of Indian, Pakistani, Bangladeshi, and Korean men of all skills. These workers were recruited by men such as Masood, the main character of the book, who charged the workers a large percentage of the wage they were to receive to get them the jobs. This was their way of life; and the workers paid because the wages they could earn in the Middle East were around eight times what they could earn at home.

The economy of most, if not all, Middle Eastern countries is centered around Oil or Black Gold and the power of the rulers of these countries is the same as their personal fortunes...immense. But there is a fine balance between the rulers, religion, and the common people; and any ruler who recklessly endangers his people, courts disaster where he and his family, if lucky, will be exiled or, at worst, be sent on a one way trip into the vastness of the hot desert and a long, slow Death in the Sun.

CHAPTER ONE
The Game Begins

"It is done Masood," said Ali as he walked in from the noisy outer office, "by now the leaders of the Arab oil world will have your demands and messages."

"Good, my friend," said Masood as he smiled, slyly. "In half an hour, the demonstration bombs will explode and they will know we mean business. Soon we'll be richer than you ever dreamed of. We have worked long and hard for this day and now it is time to relax."

The plot was simple and had been brilliantly planned and executed; it was born from a joke between Masood and Ali. Masood had enlisted the help of his old friend Kutty, a brilliant strategist, to devise a plan to manufacture and import hundreds of bombs into each of the eight richest oil-producing Middle Eastern countries. They would be planted in the foundations of government and high profile buildings during the early stages of construction and lay there as sleepers until activated by their built-in timers.

As an agent supplying Indian labour and construction workers to many sites in these countries, Masood was in the ideal position to control the plan, recruit the necessary men, and pay for their silence. Only one man knew where all the bombs were and Masood had killed him three days ago. Kutty Krishnan was that man, and the cancer which had been eating him from the inside had grown too painful for him to bear, so Masood helped end Kutty's agony with a lethal injection of heroin.

Masood would honour his promise to Kutty and in return for his help Masood would ensure Kutty's family would be well looked after when he was gone. Having spent his life as a demolition engineer, Kutty knew how to build bombs and where to put them for maximum effect.

Far away in Iran, the Shah read, with horror and disbelief, Masood's message received on his personal telex line. It said that bombs had been placed in buildings all over Iran and that a ransom of $150,000,000 had to be paid to disarm these bombs. The message stated that a demonstration explosion would take place in half an hour where a school building would be blown up; fortunately, it was Friday so the school was empty.

At exactly 12:00 noon, a deep boom, followed by a rumble, signalled the threatened destruction of the school.

Similar messages had been received in Saudi Arabia, the United Arab Emirates, Bahrain, Oman, Iraq, Libya, and Qatar, and schools in all those countries were levelled simultaneously.

Royal tempers were exploding across the Arab world as each threatened explosion ripped their peaceful, spoiled world apart. Within minutes, the telexes were chattering to each other and a news blackout was agreed upon.

In Palaces across the Arab world, leaders of the target countries despite their fury and dismay were trying to co-ordinate a response, but pride was getting in the way of who would lead the investigation and the hunt for those responsible.

"Search every building if you have to, I want these bombs found, Abdul," demanded the Shah.

"It is not possible, Highness; it would take months to check every official building, let alone the private ones, and we have only been given ninety-six hours before the next explosion. There could be hundreds of bombs in Tehran alone."

"I know that, you dolt. I also can read, but do as I say," growled the Shah glowering at everyone in the room. "We have no choice but to pay the ransom and get it back when we find those responsible. Now, arrange for the money to be paid. I will not risk any of my people being hurt or killed."

Similar conversations were going on in all the capitals with many arguing for a show of strength, but in general, the doves of peace and common good prevailed.

Back in Bombay, Masood and Ali did not need any news from anywhere to make them smile. This moment was the culmination of two years planning and work, and they knew everything had gone according to plan even before the shouting stopped and the hunt for them started.

"We must leave Bombay now," urged Masood. "Did you get the money from the bank?"

"Yes Masood. As you asked, I got dollars, francs, and sterling. Where are we going to go? Surely, there will be no hiding place for us now."

"Why should we hide Ali, my friend? Kutty has sent our instructions to London and that is where our adventure begins. Now pack, we have a flight to catch and some fun to have. I have no intentions of hiding. The messages I sent made it clear to our victims; if they hurt or kill us, their world as they know it will go up in flames. They will be surrounded by destruction and powerless to stop it, but if they pay our demand, all will be well."

"But what if they capture us and torture us, Masood?" pleaded Ali.

"Do you know where the bombs are, Ali?"

"No."

"And neither do I," smiled Masood.

"So, who the hell does and how are they disarmed?" demanded Ali impatiently.

"Patience my friend, Kutty has it all in hand," soothed Masood.

"Kutty!!! Kutty is dead."

"Yes Ali, but he arranged everything before he died. Remember, every fourth day a bomb will activate. If we are captured and tortured, we can tell them nothing so within four days there will be an explosion; they would have to release us to get the next code or...booooom, more explosions!! Now, calm down and let's get going."

Masood and Ali were soon on a plane to London at the start of the greatest adventure of either of their lives.

The whole plot was a masterstroke of genius conceived two years before, and like most great plans, its simplicity was the key. Ali had returned on leave from working in Saudi and had spent many hours complaining to his boyhood friend Masood about the treatment he received while working.

"Put a bomb under them," snapped Masood one day during a particularly long tirade from Ali.

"Now that would be fun," chuckled Ali. "But it can't be done." Ali had returned to Saudi to complete his contract and earn enough money to buy a share in Masood's recruitment business.

Meanwhile, Masood's joke had become the germ of a plan, but Masood needed help and had gone to his old friend Kutty Krishnan, a retired demolition expert. They soon became totally engrossed in the idea and as the idea grew, so did the excitement. On his next visit home a year later, Ali was amazed to find what had happened. Plans were well advanced and some of the bombs had already been placed. Masood's business had grown as well and he now had clients in all of the countries they intended to blackmail.

Once settled on the plane to London, Ali relaxed a little.

"So tell me again what happens, Masood. There is a lot to take in and my brain is not as big as yours," said Ali, looking at his friend in admiration.

"Well, Ali, we could not get a working bomb into any of the countries, so it had to go in piece by piece as machine parts; then, our men assembled them and placed them in a key part of the building, as instructed by Kutty, when the concrete was being poured."

"Yes, yes … then what?" urged Ali.

Masood sat relaxed in the first class lounge of the 747. They were alone. He had booked the whole first class section months in advance to ensure privacy.

"Give me time, Ali, have another drink. The bomb is sealed in the concrete forever. They will never find them and they sit there waiting for the activation clock to start."

"It is so clever, but once they start, how do they stop?" demanded Ali.

"That's the fun bit Ali, at least for us. They are switched off by a radio signal," answered Masood, leaving his seat and walking over to the window to watch the cotton-wool soft, clouds pass slowly below the cruising aircraft.

"So they could get turned off by accident?"

"No, the signal has to be sent within 4 hours of them being activated and it has to be a sequence of letters on a pre-set frequency."

"So who sends the message?"

"That's the fun part Ali, the Government sends it."

"This is getting stupid," snapped Ali, jumping up to join his friend at the window and shaking his head in disbelief. "How can they send a message if they don't know what to send, and if they do know what to send, they can find us and kill us at any time?"

"No, no, my friend, they do not know what to send until I tell them and I can only tell them a few hours before the explosion is due."

"So you know all the messages and all the frequencies in your head?"

"No Ali, I don't know any of them," said Masood, taking a sip of whisky from the glass he was holding.

"But..."

"Shut up Ali and let me finish. I know where to go first and where to start, after that, I will find out as we go along."

"Sounds stupid to me," replied a confused Ali, again shaking his head and returning to his chair.

"Look Ali, Kutty Krishnan set this up and we must have faith in him. He was a very clever man and planned everything. He knew he was dying and he offered to plan and arrange all the details in return for me looking after his family after he had gone. The only person who knew everything was Kutty, so we had to wait until he died before we could start the demonstration explosions. The only mistake Kutty made was living longer than he expected to; time was running out for the bombs to start activating, so I helped him with a lethal injection 3 days ago."

"You!!! You killed Kutty," challenged a surprised Ali.

"He was in great pain, Ali, and time was running out so I helped him out of his agony. If the demonstration bombs had gone off and they had caught him, all of our plans would be in ruins," Masood explained. "Now get some sleep and relax."

Several hours later having landed and passed through Heathrow Airport, Masood and Ali checked into their London hotel and settled down for the night. Meanwhile, after much argument, the security leaders of Saudi, the United Arab Emirates, Iraq, Iran, Bahrain, Oman, and Qatar had agreed on a team to find the culprits. Much to their annoyance, Libya had decided to go it alone, so the hunt was on.

Asif was from Saudi and Abdul Aziz already knew of his reputation. He was a weasel of a man, tall, thin and ugly with no soul at all and known throughout the Middle East as "The Magician." Where he went people disappeared.

From the United Arab Emirates, there was Khalaf a giant by any standard. He had a disarming smile, which showed broken rotting teeth. He was huge, very strong and loved to demonstrate his strength to anyone foolish enough to think he was a gentle giant, or to anyone who hurt any animal while he was around. He had killed a man once after he had seen him kicking a dog in the street. To Khalaf, cruelty to people was ok as long as they could stand up for themselves, but cruelty to animals made him mad and it was safer not to be around when he became mad.

Riad was from Bahrain, and was a Palestinian, surveillance and bomb specialist who had learned his trade from the British Army. He was a quiet man, happy with his own company, and often found sitting on his own reading a book. He always carried with him an old silver cigarette case with a dent at the top corner where it had stopped a bullet during a gunfight in Lebanon some years before. It was his lucky charm and he never went anywhere without it.

From Iraq came Yousef, a cruel man with a watery smile and a black heart. His only pleasure in life was the infliction of pain on anyone his masters wanted information from. He boasted he could make anyone talk and that he could make items of torture from almost any everyday item found in the average home. He left no doubt with his comrades that he meant what he said.

Oman sent Omar, a watcher, trained by the S.A.S. to hide anywhere for days, if need be, and not be spotted or found. He was a loner for the most part, and a swift and silent killer with knife or crossbow.

The man from Qatar, Swami, was a thief. If something was locked, he could open it. He was good with a knife too, as some of his victims in the past had found out to their cost. He was first class when using cameras and listening devices.

The telexes were quickly traced to Masood's office in Bombay and the frightened staff had told the police Masood and Ali had left on a business trip to London. Masood was certain they dare not kill him until he had told them everything, and he had nothing to tell them, even if they tortured him. But he did wonder how long it would be before they caught up with him and also, how long before they found out he loved pain.

He did not have long to wait with the help of the British Intelligence. One of the hunters was in a suite at the Waldorf before Ali and Masood awoke for breakfast.

CHAPTER TWO
Fun in London

Masood and Ali awoke the next day as rich men; each of the countries had to pay 150 million dollars into their numbered account. In addition, they each had to pay monthly, one percent of their respective oil revenue. Ali was awake first. It was ten o'clock on a bright sunny day in London, and he was as excited as a child.

"Come on. Time to get up, we have to eat and there's a lot to do," Ali shouted through the closed door of Masood's bedroom. "How does it feel to be so rich?"

A sleepy eyed Masood opened the door to the deafening question.

"You should know my friend. Half of it is yours."

"You are too generous Masood. I don't deserve all that."

"Yes, you do, my friend. If it had not been for you, I would not be alive. It was you who saved my life when we were children; and anyway, you gave me the idea of the bombs in the first place."

"Me! That was a joke," Ali shouted from behind his bathroom door. "I cannot believe you planned all this from a joke."

"Well, we did. Now, I am hungry, let's get breakfast," urged Masood heading for the door of the suite. Ali was through the door before realizing he had nothing on. He was so excited and busy talking, he had forgotten to dress. A disapproving glance from a passing maid brought him around and he shot back into the suite, very embarrassed. He quickly got dressed and they hurried down to breakfast.

After a huge breakfast, they went out to explore London and its famous shops. In Harrods, Ali was like a child in a toy store.

"And does Sir require anything else?" asked the assistant from behind a pile of clothes on his counter, while mentally calculating his commission.

"I think that is the lot, but I don't know how we will carry it all," mumbled Ali, slightly embarrassed by the amount he had bought.

"No problem Sir. If you tell me your address, I will have it all delivered. Did you say you were staying at The Waldorf?"

"Yes that's right, but I can't remember what suite number."

"Don't worry Sir, we can find out from them and send it all 'round."

"That's very kind," said Ali giving the man a fifty pound tip which quickly vanished into his pocket.

Masood bought a few small items, as he had plenty of clothes with him, but he did buy three new pairs of shoes. He had a thing about shoes and never went anywhere without at least, ten pairs, which he never had repaired. As soon as they showed any sign of wear or got marked, he simply gave them away and bought new ones. Ali thought it was a throwback from the days when they were children on the streets of Bombay with no shoes at all.

They returned to the hotel hours later loaded with more bags and boxes of new clothes and shoes from other shops which Ali had been attracted into. Tired, they decided on an afternoon nap. Masood woke up to find Ali in the suite lounge trying on his new clothes again.

"What shall we do after dinner, Ali?" he asked.

"I want to go out and see the West End and Soho," replied Ali.

They dined and went out to check out the famous West End. Ali marvelled at the clubs and nightlife. He had spent many a lonely night in his accommodation in Saudi dreaming of nights and times like this and now that he could touch it, smell it, and live it, he shivered with excitement.

"What shall we do first Masood; there is so much to do?"

"What do you wish for Ali? It is yours for the asking."

"I want to go in there," said Ali pointing to a brightly lit club entrance. So in they went. The doorman glared at them, but neither noticed. Just inside the door, they stood for a moment letting their eyes get used to the low lighting.

"Good evening gentlemen," said the sultry voice of a tall brunette who seemed to appear from nowhere.

"Let me show you to your seats." She led the way. Ali could not take his eyes off her hourglass figure, which he was sure had only been fitted into her tight satin dress by melting her and pouring her in. The split from the hem up the back ended just low enough to tease, but high enough to please, and he was glad to sit down,. His legs were by now, just jelly, and the bulge in his trousers was noticeable.

"What would you like to drink?" she purred.

"Champagne," said Masood.

She was back in a flash, and with a friend.

"This is Cindy," she purred again, flashing a smile of perfect white teeth surrounded by full red lips.

"And I am Mel. May we join you?" She purred as she slid into the booth next to Ali. "House rules say you're not allowed to drink alone."

"Good," said Masood. "We don't want to be alone."

"That will be £30 Sir," said the waiter who brought the champagne and four glasses.

"Is that the best you have?" asked Masood. "I only want the best." The bottle, unopened, was whisked away and another appeared with a name Masood recognized.

"Ah, Bollinger. That's better," said Masood.

"The best in the house," said the waiter. "That will be £100 Sir."

"Well, one won't last long will it? Better have one each to start." With that, Masood brought out a roll of fifty pound notes that would choke an elephant and counted out nine.

"That's one too many Sir," said the waiter.

"Just keep us happy and there's more where that came from," replied Masood, smiling.

Ali had not spoken since they sat down. He couldn't get his mouth to work at all because he had never seen anyone as gorgeous as Mel. He thought she looked great from the back but since she sat down, he had not been able to takes his gaze away from her gently, heaving breasts. He thought some of the Indian women working on Grant Road in Bombay were lovely, but in his eyes, none compared to Mel. Her dark shiny hair framed a slightly suntanned stunning face with dancing blue eyes, a fine, chiselled nose, and lips so full he felt he could rest his head on them.

Mel was clearly amused by him being dumbstruck.

"Forgive Ali, I think he has fallen in love," joked Masood, explaining. "He can speak and I am sure he will catch up with us when he has finished devouring you with his eyes."

"He is forgiven," joked Mel. "Are you in town on business or pleasure?" she asked.

"Oh definitely pleasure," said Masood. "It's our first time in London."

"Do you like what you see?" asked Cindy.

"Yes my dear," replied Masood. He certainly liked what he saw in her. Masood was good at snap assessments of people, and he had Cindy weighed up as candy coated, but hard as nails inside.

A show came on of two girls making a sad effort at a snake charming act; it looked as if they had done it a thousand times before and they, as well as the audience, had lost interest. Ali, with the help of a bottle of Bollinger, came out of his trance and found his tongue before it ended up down Mel's cleavage.

Finishing the last of the Bollinger, Masood announced he wanted something to eat and asked would the ladies join them.

"We can't," said Cindy. "We're not allowed to leave the club until it closes."

"Outrageous. Where is the manager?" demanded Masood. This brought a thin, weedy individual from behind the bar.

"Is there a problem Sir?" he asked Masood, while wringing his hands and shifting from one foot to the other.

"I would like to take these ladies out for dinner, but they say they can't go."

"That's right Sir. They are hostesses and it is their job to sit and talk to customers."

Masood rose from his seat and walked around the table towards the manager. From nowhere a huge bouncer appeared as Masood's hand went to his pocket. Thinking a knife was coming out, the bouncer stepped back to reach for a chair only to fall backwards over Ali who was crouching on the floor behind him. Before anyone else could react, Ali was on the bouncer's chest with a flick knife at his throat.

"Don't move, for God's sake don't move," said Masood. "Ali put the knife down please. He wasn't going to hurt me, were you?"

The bouncer carefully, in a hoarse whisper, got out the word.

"No."

Ali let the man get up; the bewildered bouncer couldn't believe a man only five feet tall had done that to him.

"I was only getting some money out," said Masood, explaining his reaching for his pocket.

"Money for what?" asked the manager, who was now ashen coloured after seeing his protector so easily dealt with.

"As I said, we want the ladies to go out with us and I thought if I paid you, they could leave," answered Masood.

"How much did you have in mind?" said the manager, smirking and wringing his hands even faster than before.

"This much," said Masood producing the rest of the elephant choking bundle. The manager's greedy eyes bulged briefly before he snatched the bundle from Masood's open hand.

"Certainly Sir, and I hope you have a nice evening. Cindy, Mel, please show the gentlemen what London has to offer."

As they left the club and got into a taxi, Masood noticed the bouncer glaring at Ali and could not resist going back to whisper in his ear.

"He would have cut your throat without a thought."

In the cab Ali reached for Mel's hand. She was shaking.

"Don't worry, I wasn't in any danger," Ali assured her.

"Don't worry!!! I've seen George smash men up for no reason, but no one ever got the better of him before. Is what Masood said true, would you have killed him?"

"If, he had hurt my friend, yes," replied Ali.

"God I'm glad you're on my side tonight."

"So am I," said Ali.

They drove around London in the taxi for an hour with the girls pointing out the sights.

"We must come back and do this in the daytime," said Ali. "I want my picture taken sitting on one of those lions in Trafalgar Square."

They ended up on The Strand at a restaurant that one of the girls recommended. They all ate ravenously and the wine flowed freely. When it came time to leave, Masood produced another huge bundle of notes and paid the bill. Their waiter thought Christmas had come early when Masood pressed a hundred pound tip into his hand as they left. No one asked if the girls were going back to Masood and Ali's hotel, it was just assumed they were.

"I am dying to know..." began Cindy in the taxi back to the hotel, "how much did you give the weasel?"

"Who is the weasel?" asked Masood.

"Jim, the manager of the club," replied Cindy.

"Oh him, well the bundle had five thousand pounds in it and I spent four hundred and fifty on the champagne, so I suppose just over four and a half thousand pounds," said Masood casually

"That's a fortune, just to take us out to dinner!" exclaimed Cindy.

"It's only money, plenty more where that came from," replied Masood.

Arriving at The Waldorf, they went straight up to their suite.

The girls were impressed. Masood, without asking, rang room service and ordered more champagne.

"It will be cheaper here than at the club," said Mel.

"Yes I know I was ripped off, but who cares, we're here now and having a good time."

"What do you do for a living, it must be well paid?" asked Cindy. "I have met some rich Arabs, but none who spend like you."

"Oh you could say we're in demolition," answered Masood. Ali collapsed on one of the settees laughing hysterically.

"What's up with him?" asked Cindy.

"I think he just got the joke," said Masood.

"What joke?" asked Cindy.

"Oh it's a private one I may tell you one day if you stay around long enough," replied Masood. He suddenly realized there was music playing and turned to find Ali dancing with Mel. It looked quite funny. She was tall, and his total five feet put his head at her bust level and he was making the most of his opportunity.

"Want to dance?" he asked.

"No, let's leave them to it," replied Cindy, taking Masood by the hand and heading for one of the bedrooms. Masood smiled and a tingle of anticipation ran down his spine. He hoped the rest of the time in London was going to be as good as tonight had been up to now, and promised to be until morning. The music was still playing as he gently closed the door. Once in the bedroom, Cindy headed for the bathroom and Masood waited, relaxed on a deep comfy settee. She was not long and when she emerged, she was worth the wait. She was only wearing a black thong, and her pert breasts did not move in the four strides of her long legs as she crossed the room and was by his side.

He playfully slapped her bare thigh and she slapped him hard across the face.

"Don't slap me," she snarled, taking him completely by surprise. "I don't let anyone slap me."

Masood went red.

"I'm so sorry. I was just being playful."

"That's ok. I'm just funny about being roughed up. You get a lot of strange men in the club, who think they can take liberties because they pay over the odds for the drinks."

"Let's start again," he said, rising from his position and taking her in his strong arms. They kissed like lovers who have not enjoyed each other for a long time. When the kiss was over she had expertly stripped him of all but his shoes and socks. A fact which turned them both into fits of giggling. Their passion that night knew no bounds until they both collapsed exhausted on the bed.

In the other half of the suite, Ali and Mel had ended their dance and passion had taken over. They left the music on as they kissed, and left a trail of clothes on the way to Ali's bedroom.

"I have been away from a woman for a long time…" he told Mel "so please be gentle with me."

"I will Ali, I will," she purred to him as they sank onto the bed.

He may only have been small in stature, but he was built like a bull elephant where it mattered. She reached for him, and they both gasped together, her in surprise, he in pure enjoyment. He was the one who was rough, but she knew why and would tame him later. His stamina surprised and pleased her and his knowledge of a woman's body was amazing, but even he tired in the end and they fell into a deep satisfied sleep.

They spent the next three days together seeing more of the sights, with Ali having his photo taken in some of the strangest places including, sitting on the top of a lion in Trafalgar Square. They got to know each other better along the way.

"Where do you come from in India, Ali?" asked Mel.

"I was born in Bombay. My family was very poor, and I started my working life when I was six polishing people's shoes and running errands."

"That must have been hard," said Mel.

"It was but no more than most other boys of my age. It was work or starvation, and I wasn't going to starve." Ali's face darkened as he remembered back to those dark days of his childhood and the daily fight to survive.

"And have you known Masood all your life?"

"Most of it. We met at school and soon became great friends, but he is the clever one. He has always had a bigger brain than me, that's why he started his recruitment company and I only worked for him."

"Oh that's where his money comes from. It must be a massive company for him to be so wealthy."

"Not really," Ali started to say before Masood cut in.

"What are you doing boring Mel with all those silly details? I thought we had come out to see the sights," said Masood, flashing Ali an annoyed glance.

"What about some lunch? I'm starving and the Savoy Grill is just over there."

Once inside the girls went to powder their noses.

"What the hell do you think you were doing Ali? We can't get into too much detail with Mel and Cindy at this stage or they will want to know where our money comes from, and that could be the last we see of them."

"Sorry Masood, I wasn't thinking."

"No, you can say that again. If they ask any more, just keep things general and for God's sake don't go into any detail about how we got our money," chided Masood.

"What's this about money?" asked Cindy appearing at Masood's left shoulder.

"Nothing really, just telling Ali he shouldn't go on about money to try to impress you or Mel."

"Quite right, we're not those sorts of girls," she laughed. "Now, did we come in here to eat or just spend a penny?"

Masood was already handing out the menus.

"So where were we Ali? Ah yes, you were telling me about you and Masood becoming friends."

"It's boring really Mel. I would rather hear about you and Cindy."

"Oh, well if you two want to remain all dark and mysterious, Cindy and I met at the club some years back, but we haven't always worked there. We moved about a bit but always seem to go back there in the end and we have lots of friends there."

They continued to talk over the meal with the girls revealing some of the services provided at the club. Mel then said that there have been a number of odd clients which caused much giggling by the girls. Then Ali butted in.

"Tell us about them then."

"Well, there is this bloke who we know is a judge because we've seen him in the papers. He does big trials at the Old Bailey," Mel went on.

"And," cut in Ali.

"Give me chance. Well, he comes in regular as clockwork every Thursday. He always drinks scotch, but insists it has to be out of Jill's shoes!"

"Dirty old sod," jumped in Masood.

"Well, Jill, she keeps a pair of plastic shoes special for him."

"Anyone else?" asked Masood.

"Oh yes," said Cindy. "We have a couple who are really weird. They come in every now and again and just start dancing in front of everyone."

"What's so weird about that?" asked Ali.

"Give me chance to finish," urged Cindy. "Then they start to strip each other off and do it in front of everyone there on the dance floor."

"Do what?" asked a bemused Ali.

"For God's sake Ali, do you need a picture?" jumped in Mel.

"Oh! Oh that," replied an embarrassed Ali, turning a nice shade of red. The girls went on with several more stories during the rest of the meal and on the way back to the hotel.

It was on the evening of the third day, that Ali pointed out to Masood they had followers.

"What shall we do Masood?"

"Nothing for now, they have not tried to harm us, and if they wanted to capture us, they could have done so any time in the last two days," answered Masood.

"What do you mean the last two days?" demanded Ali.

"That is how long ago I saw them," replied Masood.

"You bastard! Why did you not say something?" fumed Ali.

"Because you would only have worried as you are doing now, and where would that get us?" replied Masood in a calming voice.

"We shall have to run," urged Ali.

"Run Ali! Run where? They would find us easily, and anyway they can't afford to hurt us," said Masood.

"Has anyone told them that? And what about the girls?" asked an increasingly irate Ali.

It was a good question. Masood had not planned to get involved with anyone, but Cindy was special and over the last three days and nights, he had found his instinct to be right. She knew how to be cruel in ways that only someone who has suffered themselves could possibly know. She brought just the right amount of pain into their lovemaking that brought it to perfection for him and taught him what she wanted most from him.

CHAPTER THREE
Watching the Prey

"We have found out who the culprits are, Highness," announced Abdul Aziz, security advisor to the Shah, as he entered the room. "They are two Indian nationals, a Masood Jaleel and Ali Beg. They are staying at The Waldorf in London, at the moment. I have my best man watching them. Shall we bring them back here for questioning?"

"No you idiot, they are not to be harmed, at least not yet. We have yet to see if they come through with the code to switch off the first bomb and then we will try to find a way around what they have done. Patience is our best course of action," snapped Shah Reza.

"Yes, Highness. Meanwhile, the other agents have arrived here and I suggest they all travel to London to join Captain Saeed and follow Jaleel and Beg while we work out what is to be done."

"Do not bother me with the details, Abdul. Just do it and make sure they are not harmed," said the Shah as he waved his arms in dismissal.

"Yes, Highness," said Abdul. His smile of triumph had now gone and he was glad to leave the room. He had rarely seen the Shah in such a mood and was glad to be out of his way. Many thought the Shah a kindly man, but he had his bad side and when he was in a bad mood it was best not to be around. Abdul went straight to the part of the Palace where the agents were waiting. There were six men in all, Libya still going it alone.

"Welcome gentlemen. I am Abdul Aziz and I will be in charge of this operation. My second in command, Captain Saeed, will meet you in London and lead you on this mission. Your instructions, for now, are to travel to London and watch the two men we are after, but they are not to be touched or harmed. If anyone else tries to harm them, you are to use whatever force you feel necessary to stop them. We need to know what their plans are so this may be a long assignment. I repeat, do not interfere with them in any way unless they are in danger. Lastly, just to complicate matters, the Libyans are acting on their own. If they get in the way, despatch them. Am I clear?" All the men in the room nodded their heads in understanding and left.

Within an hour, they were on a flight to London. Upon arrival, they were met by an official from the Foreign Office and Captain Saeed. The official, a weedy little man with very bad breath, and only a few wisps of hair, welcomed them and issued them with special papers giving diplomatic immunity.

"Her Majesty's Government hopes there will be no trouble in our country, but if there is, we don't really want to know. We have a basic idea of what has happened and will help if we can, but for the most part you are on your own and our people will not interfere. Your weapons, etc can be collected from the Iranian Embassy. Have a nice, but hopefully, short stay gentlemen."

With that, he was gone and glad to be out of it, as they looked and smelled like a nasty bunch. He was glad not to be involved.

They travelled in two taxis to The Waldorf where Masood and Ali were staying. On arrival, they settled down in two suites directly under Masood and Ali's suite.

The next day a letter arrived for Masood. He did not have it sent to the suite, choosing to collect it himself from reception. He made sure he was alone when he read it in the bar. It was from his old friend, Kutty, and was short and to the point.

"My friend, by the time you read this, I will, as you know be dead. Your instructions and the codes required to disarm the first device are set out below, so you must get this information to the security officer at the Saudi Embassy in London. As long as they follow my instructions nothing can go wrong. If they don't, then God help you all. You and Ali have always wanted to travel the world, you can now do this. Your next stop is Paris and your next instructions will be given to you in four days' time. Good luck my friend, have a long and prosperous life."

The first page ended with instructions of the hotel in Paris where they were to stay.

On the second page, was a set of instructions for the embassy official. The instructions named Jubail, a port town in Saudi, where the radio message must be broadcast from, the frequency, a time and date, and a series of letters to be sent in Morse code. Masood pocketed the letter and returned to the suite.

"Right everyone," he announced, as he entered the suite. "Tomorrow we are off to Paris." Ali was surprised, but the girls were dumbstruck.

"We can't do that, we have our jobs to go back to. Jim will kill us if we don't go back soon," protested Mel. She had feared this moment and the tears began to well up in her eyes.

"What do you mean Jim will kill you?" snapped Ali.

"It's only a figure of speech Ali, but we do have to earn a living," Cindy joined in.

Ali suddenly realized they knew very little about Mel or Cindy's lives. Did they have family? Where do they live?

"I can fix things with Jim," boasted Masood. "I will pay him what you call a golden handshake."

Cindy burst out laughing. "No Masood, it is the person leaving that gets the golden handshake." Confused, Masood shook his head.

"But can you, and will you, come to Paris?" pleaded Ali. He stood with his head down, looking like a little boy who has just lost his favourite toy.

"We don't know. What is this all about and when will we be back?" asked Mel.

"I am not sure when or even if we will be back. All I can promise is it will be a great adventure and you can come back to England at any time you are unhappy," promised a desperate Masood.

"We need to talk about this Masood," said Mel.

"Fine," he said, as he settled down on a deep comfy sofa.

"No! Not all of us, just Cindy and me."

"Oh and what shall we do?" asked Ali.

"Go down to the bar and have a drink. We will find you when we're ready with our decision."

Leaving the suite, Ali and Masood headed for the bar.

"What do you think Masood, will they come? I hope so. I have never met anyone like Mel."

"No," said Masood. "And if you drool any more over her she will slip on it one day and break her lovely neck."

"Am I really that bad Masood?"

"Yes Ali, but it's not a crime to be in love."

"But what about our plans, won't the girls mess things up or tie us down? And what about the cost?"

"Ali, dear Ali, always the worrier, we have over a billion dollars in the bank and more to come. I think we can afford the extra air tickets and anything else we want. I have already arranged a little surprise for the girls if they agree to come with us."

By the time the girls came down to the bar, Ali was very drunk. He was clearly worried they may not agree to come to Paris and had hit the bottle hard; he was talking Masood's ears off.

"Thank goodness you're here. He is driving me mad. Have you made your mind up?"

"Yes we have, and we would love to come with you, but there is only one problem."

"And whachhh's that," slurred Ali, slipping off his stool onto the floor in a heap.

"How do we get back if you get tired of us or we fall out?" asked Mel.

"Ah," said Masood. "I think I have the answer to that but first, we must go and see Jim at the club. We have a golden handshake to sort out."

Bemused, Mel and Cindy helped Ali to the taxi and they all travelled to the club. George, the bouncer, was on the door and not happy to see any of them.

"Miss the money Cindy," he sneered, as they walked past him.

"Get stuffed George," she snapped, sneering back at him and walking on in. They found a table and waited for the waiter. Instead, Jim came over.

"Sorry we missed work a few nights Jim," said Mel.

"Not a problem Mel. Up to you if you come in or not," replied Jim with a sickly smile.

This baffled Mel and Cindy. Was Jim ill? He was usually a sarcastic bastard at the best of times, and not averse to slapping the girls about if they got lippy or let him down.

"I'm seeing you in a different light tonight Jim, you feeling alright?"

"Not a different light Cindy, just from a different position, if you know what I mean."

"No, I don't bloody know what you mean," she challenged. Cindy took shit from no one and even Jim didn't slap her, ever.

"Perhaps I can clear things up," interjected Masood, beaming all over his face.

"Be bloody great if shhhomeone could," slurred Ali resting his head on the table.

"From now on Jim, you are to take your instructions from Mel and Cindy."

"Certainly Mr Jaleel," replied Jim. The silence around the table could be cut with a blunt knife until Ali drunkenly mimicked Masood.

"From now on Jiiiimmm you take instructionsss from Cel and Mindy ok." Jim went a little red, but Masood waived at Ali.

"Shut up you drunken bum." That broke the silence.

"What are you on about Masood, this is not funny? We know you have a strange sense of humour, but if you think I'm going away with a sick sod like you you're mistaken," jumped in Cindy.

"Sorry Cindy, it was meant to be a surprise, but it came out all wrong," said Masood.

"What surprise?" Cindy asked. "I don't understand. Do you know what he is on about Mel? If you do, for God's sake tell me," she urged.

"It's obvious you silly cow," replied Mel. "Somehow, Masood owns a share in the club and made us managers over Jim." Masood laughed and Ali started giggling.

"Oh, so I'm wrong and this is some sort of joke," snapped Mel.

"No you're wrong, but it's not a joke," said Masood pulling from his pocket a folded sheaf of paper. "All you two have to do is sign on the dotted line and the club is yours." Cindy's jaw dropped so far it nearly hit the floor. Mel went one better and did hit the floor in a dead faint.

"Get some water Jim," snapped Masood. Ali, who had missed much of the last few minutes asleep, woke up, saw Mel on the floor, and was up on his feet swaying drunkenly and looking for a fight with whoever hit Mel.

"It's ok Ali, she just fainted."

"Shhhomm people can't take their drink," Ali slurred and collapsed in a drunken heap next to Mel. It took some time after they brought Mel around, for her and Cindy to grasp what had just happened. Masood explained it was his way of ensuring they could leave him and Ali at any time, and were with them because they wanted to be, not just for the money.

They picked Ali up off the floor and Masood carried him from the club. As they left, Cindy stopped in the doorway. Leaning over, she whispered something in Masood's ear. He smiled and nodded.

"George you're fired," said Cindy.

"Who the fuck do you think you are slut," replied George.

"Your new boss and you're still fired." Masood guessed what was coming and in a flash was between Cindy and George, but the punch aimed at Cindy never arrived. George collapsed like a burst balloon onto the pavement felled by a punch to the back of the neck from Khalaf, who smiled his rotten toothed smile and walked away.

"Who the fuck was that?" screeched Mel.

"Don't know," said Masood, "but he seemed a nice man and he obviously didn't like George."

George groaned as if to agree, but they left him where he was and got into the waiting taxi.

"The Waldorf please driver," announced Masood placing Ali carefully in the cab.

"If he's sick, gov, it's extra," said the cabby.

"If he's sick, I'll buy you a new cab," said Masood.

The driver never got his new cab. Ali waited until they were in the suite, and then made a dash for the bathroom, and it was some time before he emerged looking the worse for wear and ready for bed. Mel went with him, but she did not sleep. So much had happened in the last few days, but the events of the last few hours were like something out of a dream and she kept pinching herself to make sure she was not dreaming.

Cindy didn't sleep either and she was determined Masood wasn't going to sleep until he had answered all her questions.

"Do you make a habit of picking up girls and buying clubs for them Masood?"

"No, only the ones I really like," he teased. She slapped him for that and he knew the night was going to be an interesting one. By morning, with a bit of luck, he would be black and blue.

"So what happened, Khalaf?" demanded Saeed, the team leader.

"Nothing really, they went to this club and I waited outside while Riad followed them in. They came out after a while and spoke to the doorman. I did not hear what was said, but it was turning nasty and the doorman went to hit Jaleel," replied Khalaf.

"Yes, yes, and what happened?" demanded Saeed.

"I dealt with it. Our instructions are, he is not to be hurt and I made sure he wasn't," said an offended Khalaf.

"Yes, but did you speak to them? demanded a confused Saeed.

"No, I just left and let them get into a taxi," replied Khalaf.

"Hamdulla thanks God for that. They know we are here, but at least he was not hurt," said a relieved Saeed.

The next morning, Masood rose early and, leaving an exhausted Cindy in bed, went off to the Saudi Embassy. On arrival, he asked to see the senior security officer and was shown to a side room. After about ten minutes, the officer appeared and asked his business, which Masood explained. But half way through, the man cut him short, excused himself, and left the room. Masood opened the door to look outside only to find two guards blocking his exit.

It seemed an eternity, but was only about fifteen minutes before the man returned with another man in very regal Arab dress.

"I am Prince Faisal and I wish to talk to you," he said as he entered the room. "We have been awaiting some form of contact from you, but we wish to know what, apart from money, are your motives for doing this to our country."

"I have no other motives Highness," replied Masood. "I am a business-man with information for sale."

"Yes, but you now know that we know who you and your friend are and we can take and torture you at any time."

"Yes, Highness, we are aware of that, and I thank your man for his help last night. But you must also be aware that if you torture us and fail, or kill us, then hundreds of buildings, some official, some private, throughout the oil producing Arab world will be destroyed, and you will be powerless to stop it."

"We will see, we will see," said Prince Faisal, trying to hide his anger with a smile. "You have something for me I believe?"

Masood handed Prince Faisal a paper with the instructions, which he read silently.

"You may leave for now, but we may meet again and next time I may not be so pleasant."

Masood left the Embassy and returned to The Waldorf where he found Cindy and Mel chatting excitedly, and Ali hiding under the bedcovers.

"Good morning Ali."

"Do not shout Masood my head will burst. Those two in there have been shouting all morning."

"I'm not shouting and it's your own fault for getting drunk. I have booked the tickets. We are on the four o'clock flight to Paris. Our work here is done."

"You have been to the Embassy. Did they not question you or try to arrest you?"

"Ali! Dear Ali! When will you realize they have to protect us, not hurt us, and that was demonstrated outside the club last night?"

"What club?"

"The night club I gave to the girls."

"Oh, that's what they have been chattering like monkeys about all morning."

"Yes my friend, now get dressed. I am hungry and we will have to leave for the airport soon."

In their suite close by, Saeed and Swami sat listening to the speaker picking up Masood's conversation from the bug in his shoes.

"So they are off to Paris. That bug you planted works well, Swami. I have booked four of us on the same flight. The rest will catch the next flight and we will all meet at the hotel."

"I understand from Prince Faisal that Jaleel took the first set of instructions to the Embassy this morning," said Asif.

"Good," replied Saeed. "Then the game is on and I am looking forward to having some fun with Jaleel and his little friend in the future."

"What do you mean we leave for Paris in two hours? We don't have a thing to wear," protested Mel.

"Typical woman," replied Masood. "What's wrong with the clothes you have?"

"Typical, man's reply. If we're going to be seen in the best places, we have to have the right clothes," said Cindy.

"Well, we haven't got time to buy anything now, but if the clothes that I had delivered while we were at breakfast will do for now, we will buy you a new wardrobe in Paris."

"What clothes?" asked Mel.

"The ones on the beds," replied Masood.

With shrieks of excitement, the girls headed for the bedrooms.

CHAPTER FOUR
Adventure in Paris

How they made the flight, Ali did not know. Cindy and Mel took ages to choose what they were wearing, but when they emerged from the bedroom they looked stunning. Ali could not believe he was so lucky.

"I have never flown first class," said Mel. "There is so much room and what service! It's certainly the only way to travel."

"Yes, and that's the way it will be from now on ladies," announced Ali. As he spoke, he puffed out his chest which made them all laugh.

Saeed and his men were not so happy. They were in economy as these were the only seats left at such short notice and it felt cramped. Fortunately for them, it was a short flight and they were soon landing at Charles de Gaulle airport where they were met by an embassy car which followed Masood and Ali to The Hilton in Paris.

"We must go up the Eiffel Tower," announced Cindy.

"Not me," said Ali. "I hate heights."

"Me too," said Mel, winking at Ali. The only high thing she wanted to get on was his manhood when he was lying down.

"Let's get some rest," suggested Masood. "We have a busy night ahead of us and I don't want anyone falling asleep."

"An afternoon nap would be nice," agreed Ali quickly. He grabbed Mel's hand and headed for one of the bedrooms of the suite. Mel was just as keen. She knew exactly what Ali had in mind and it wasn't sleep, at least, not straight away.

"Sex mad," said Masood.

"Yes," agreed Cindy. "Can't understand why," she laughed heading for the other bedroom.

She and Masood were getting to know each other well and she loved his foreplay. He loved the way she was cruel to him to make him lust for her lithe body. She was slim but not skinny with pert breasts, and small brown nipples which he loved to play with. His attention drove her wild. He would allow his slippery tongue to tantalize her on the way down to her mound which was well covered with a mass of fine hair. His first touch of her lips with his teasing tongue always made her gasp, then he would settle into a gentle rhythm making her want to climb the walls with pleasure, while she dug her long nails into his back making him work harder, until the explosion blew her mind and she found she was so tense she could not move her legs.

They lay together for a while until she had recovered, then she was off the bed in a bound and back just as quickly. In her hand was a belt and on her hands were gloves, which were made for handling steel. They were too big for her, but that did not matter. They were black with a coating of metal bits on the outside to protect the wearer from being cut when handling sharp or rough steel in the steel factories.

He lay face down at first, not sure where she would start this time. Although, so excited by now he felt her first touch would bring an orgasm, it was not to be. She raked his back with her gloved hand before three blows with the belt on his bare buttocks brought tears to his eyes.

"Turn over you baby," she ordered. He obeyed without protest.

"What do you want?" she demanded.

He already knew better than to answer.

"If you don't tell me, I can't please you," she cooed. He stayed silent because he knew it drove her mad and the madder she got the greater his thrill.

"Come on you bastard," she was getting annoyed now. He was looking forward to what was coming and he wasn't going to make it too quick or easy. His erection felt like he was going to burst and she smiled a wicked smile.

"Cindy knows what you want," she said, grasping his manhood in her gloved hand and squeezing. The pain was sensational as she tried to lift him from the bed, it seemed for a moment she would tear it out at the root, but she let go and he gasped.

"Oh! Liked that did you?" He smiled as she sat astride him and rubbed his chest with the rough gloves. "Now, I will ride you until you cry for mercy," and she did. He exploded inside her in seconds, but she would not stop until she was satisfied as well. Then, she rolled off onto the giant bed.

She was asleep in minutes, but he just lay there with a pulsing groin. She was the best lover he had ever had and he hoped she would stay a long time.

Ali and Mel, having enjoyed each other, had fallen asleep and were woken up by Masood knocking at the bedroom door and saying he was hungry.

"Is he always like this?" asked Mel.

"Yes, he eats like a horse," said Ali.

"Oh and you're hung like one," she laughed teasing his size.

"Is that a complaint madam?" Ali asked, with a big grin on his face.

"Not from me Sir," she replied. She also had a grin like a cat that has just had the cream, which she had earlier!

"Let's eat," he said.

"You just did," she said. "Or wasn't I enough for you?" said Mel still grinning.

"I could do with seconds," he said remembering how she tasted and making a lunge for her but she was ready and off the bed and out of reach, laughing on the way to the shower. The last words he heard before the sound of the shower drowned her out were.

"Maybe later tiger," He could wait.

They dined at the Lido de Paris. The show is world famous, and they enjoyed great food and the magnificence of the show. None of them had seen the like of it before and little was said during the evening, each of them lost in their own world of enjoyment. The girls were enthralled by the music and wonderful costumes, Masood and Ali by the constant parade of beauty and grace of the show. For most of the show, the ladies' costumes were topless, but it was not just the constant parade of bare breasts that kept the audience enthralled. The show was spectacular by any standard; the speed with which sets were changed, the elegant costumes and head dresses of multi-coloured ostrich feathers were magnificent and a wonder to behold. It brought home to Cindy and Mel the seediness of the club they now owned.

It was late when they returned to the hotel and they were all tired. With little banter, they all retired and sleep was soon upon them all.

It was a lazy morning in Paris when they woke, but after a good breakfast they were off shopping on the Champs Elysees. Mel and Cindy were like two children, in and out of the shops and stores chattering and laughing.

"Are you sure you're not bored Ali?" Mel asked.

"No I am enjoying myself. I have never been shopping with a woman before and it is fascinating," replied Ali, pretending to yawn and getting a playful dig in the ribs for his cheek.

"And you, Masood?" asked Cindy.

"I like seeing you enjoy yourself and I love to spend money on you my love."

The same did not apply to Yousef and Omar who were on protection and following duty. This was a source of amusement to Ali and Masood. They, of course, had not told the girls of the situation, not wishing to worry or upset them. It was not long before they had more clothes than they could all carry and a return to the hotel was made for lunch. After lunch, Ali and Masood had a nap while the girls again tried on everything they had bought. There was a lot of giggling and laughing coming from the bug in the suite and it was starting to get to Swami.

"Damn women why do they have to make so much noise. Can't we turn it off?" Swami snapped.

"No," replied Saeed. "If we do, we may miss a vital conversation between Masood and Ali, and the sooner they give themselves away the sooner we can have some fun of our own. I promise you when that day comes, you can pick one of the women and do what you like with her. Will that keep you from moaning?"

"Now that's worth waiting for," sneered Swami. "I could have a lot of fun with Ali's girlfriend." Even Yousef shuddered at that thought. Swami was slimy; the sort of man to make your skin crawl and make you count your fingers after you shook hands with him. His black eyes showed no feelings; he was a creep in every sense of the word.

They spent four wonderful days in Paris, seeing the sights and after much persuasion, going up the Eiffel Tower.

"This is wonderful," said Cindy. "I can see so far."

"I'm not looking," said a very nervous Mel, nearly crushing Ali's arm with the tightness of her grip. Ali was putting a brave face on it but he did not like heights and had come close to losing his job in the Middle East a few times when he had refused to go up the high rise buildings.

"This really is fantastic," agreed Masood. "I have arranged for us to have dinner here tonight at Altitude 95, the restaurant at the top of the first lift. It's called that because its ninety-five metres above the ground."

"Oh I'm glad it's not the one near the top," said Mel. "I couldn't eat anything if it was."

"I thought so, that's why I booked this one," confirmed Masood.

On the way down, it was Ali who was sick in the lift. He tried to hold it back but in the end, the speed of the lift was too much for the contents of his stomach and it made no difference that he had his eyes closed. Luckily, Cindy saw it coming and emptied her handbag onto the floor just in time to catch most of it. Unfortunately, the smell from Ali and the motion of the lift started a chain reaction, and by the time the lift stopped it was awash with contributions from nearly everyone.

It put the lift out of action for some time while it was cleaned out. Ali was so ill, all he wanted to do was go back to the hotel.

"I am so embarrassed," he confessed in the taxi on the way to the hotel.

"Don't worry Ali, you were the first, but not the last," said Masood laughing. "Shall we still go back tonight?" he asked.

"Let's see how we all feel after a rest this afternoon," suggested Cindy.

They did return in the evening and had a wonderful meal.

Ali chose Dublin Bay prawns with a chili dip, as did Cindy. Masood and Mel went for the Parma ham and melon. Ali's face, when the prawns were served set up in full shell in a fighting stance around the plate, was a picture to behold.

All thoughts about the height of the restaurant were forgotten as they ate, drank, and chattered.

For the main course, Ali and Masood chose beef with a peppery sauce, this being a speciality of the chef. Mel went for veal and Cindy decided on chicken in a mild mustard sauce.

"It is a strange place to have a restaurant," said Mel. "Having steelwork all around and the girders as part of the décor, but it works well and I feel safe."

"Yes," agreed Cindy. "It is strange but I know what you mean, it gives you a sense of security seeing all this massive metal about the place."

The rest of the evening passed in quiet conversation and on return to the hotel they all went to the suite.

"I am tired," said Ali winking at Mel. She yawned in agreement. "We will see you two in the morning."

"Mattress in for another bashing Ali?" said Masood.

"No," Ali protested, to no avail.

"Just keep the noise down. You woke up half of Paris last night."

"Yes, and you two woke up the other half," defended Mel. It was a different Ali that Mel saw that night. He was still embarrassed from being sick and she had to persuade him that it was alright, and she did not think any the less of him for it, or think of him as less of a man. Their lovemaking was gentle as she stroked his hairless chest, working her way down to his steadily rousing manhood.

She lowered her head until her lips were brushing the tip then flicked her tongue gently back and forth while he gently gasped his appreciation. She looked down to see his toes curling and uncurling as she brought him closer to that heavenly moment of release, but she teased him knowing he would not want it to end too soon. Time and time again she expertly brought him close, only to ease away and let his urgency subside. When she finally climaxed him, he thought his head would explode at the same time as his groin did.

Now it was her turn and he was going to make her wait, as she had made him wait. She lay back and he looked down on her and wondered what such a gorgeous woman was doing with him. He started by teasing her erect nipples, squeezing and nibbling them. In turn, he knew that drove her insane. Then his tongue travelled slowly down to her love tunnel, never actually arriving, always turning back before touching her aching clitoris. The first time he made contact, she thought she would die from pleasure, his teasing and tantalising lifting her to heights she had never known before; then he was lapping at her, and she could feel herself getting heated as never before. By now, she had a hold of the bed headboard and was digging her nails in. She felt two of them break, but she did not care. She was on her way to heaven and nothing was going to stop her getting there. When she finally came, the sea crashed and the drums roared. She had her hands on his back now and tore at his flesh until he cried out. It went on forever, or at least it seemed like forever, until she heard his voice through the red mist.

"Mel! Mel my love, you're hurting me."

She let go and he rolled away, blood streaming down his back. He was obviously in pain.

"Oh my God, Ali what have I done?"

"It is nothing," he protested. He tried in vain to hide the pain he was feeling.

She burst into tears.

"What have I done?"

He was beside her now holding her gently and whispering that it would be alright. They lay together for a while before she rose to go the bathroom.

"Oh my God, Ali I have hurt you so much."

"It is nothing my love, honestly," he protested.

"Look at the bed."

He did and for the first time, saw how much blood he had lost. By now, she was distraught and it was all he could do to console her at all.

"Honestly, it doesn't hurt as much as you think." She spent a lot of time bathing his back until he fell into a restless sleep.

In the morning while Ali and Masood were in their respective bathrooms, Mel went to Cindy and told her what had happened.

"It will be alright Mel. Ali loves you and he has said its ok."

"I did not mean to hurt him and now I feel so bad, but at the time, it was so fantastic I didn't know what I was doing."

"If I know Ali, he would be so proud to hear you say that, that he would not care if you had torn his head off."

"Who wouldn't mind if she tore his head off," interjected Masood, coming out of the bathroom. Cindy explained it all to Masood while Mel cried.

"There, there," he comforted her. "Cindy is right. Ali would be so proud; he would not even notice any pain, honestly."

Mel returned to their bedroom to find Ali lying on the bed. The curtains were still drawn and the room was in semi darkness. Ali looked towards the door as Mel entered.

"Are you alright my love?" he asked.

"Yes, I just went to speak to Cindy for a while."

"Was it about last night?"

"Yes it was. How did you know?"

"They are right you know. I am proud of last night," he smiled.

"You! You were listening at the door."

"Yes my love that's what doors are for?" He smiled again and she could not be angry.

They had a lot of fun in Paris, known as the city of love, but Ali was already in love before he came to Paris. He hoped Mel felt the same about him. He was not sure though, she was deep and did not show her true feelings readily. Even Cindy did not know the answer to that one either, and she had known Mel for a long time.

"I love you Mel." The words came out of Ali's mouth before he could stop them, as they lay in bed on their last night in Paris.

"I know you do Ali," she replied.

"How do you know? What I just said was a surprise even to me."

"A woman knows these things, I don't know how, we just do."

"And do you feel the same?"

"I think so my love, but I need a little time to be sure."

Ali thought his heart would burst. He wanted to jump up and tell the world, but she pulled him close and held him tight. This was to be their secret for now until she was sure, and then he could tell the universe. Their lovemaking was gentle that night. Tenderness replaced passion until they fell into a gentle slumber.

Mel did not wake when Ali left the room during the night, nor did she wake when he returned a short time later.

In the morning, after breakfast, Masood received a letter by messenger. He excused himself and went to the bedroom to make a phone call. He no longer had to visit any Embassy to pass on the information. Prince Faisal had given him a list of direct numbers to call with further instructions as and when he was ready. On his return from the bedroom, Masood announced they were leaving that afternoon.

"We like it here," Mel and Cindy protested.

"So do we," replied Masood. "But we have business to deal with and we must go. You can stay if you wish, but Ali and I must leave today."

There was a knock at the door. Masood answered it to find a waiter with an envelope on a tray.

"Ah," said Masood taking the envelope, "our tickets." He tipped the waiter and then closed the door.

"Where are we going Masood?" asked Ali.

"Dubai," was his only reply as he entered the bedroom and closed the door behind him. Ali burst in.

"This is madness. We are going to stay in a country we are blackmailing money from."

"Calm down Ali! Calm down, they will not touch us. If anything, they'll protect us, at least for now, and you did say you wanted to travel the world."

"How do you know we have to go to Dubai?" demanded Ali.

"It was in the note this morning," replied Masood.

"And who was the note from?" demanded Ali.

"It was from Kutty," replied Masood.

"It can't be. He is dead."

"Yes, yes, but he set all this up before he died and he was a very clever man," said Masood.

"That's creepy," said Ali with a visible shudder.

"At last a break," exclaimed Saeed.

"So they get their instructions by letter, and the next one will be delivered in Dubai. At least we can intercept that one and read the contents before they do. Then we can get our hands on them and find out the whole plan. It seems our friends are not as smart as they think. It's a shame really. I had hoped they would be more of a challenge than this."

"I am not so sure," said Omar. "Masood said the organiser was a clever man. It's too easy, too soon, if you ask me."

"I didn't," snapped Saeed. His eyes flashed with anger.

"We will see," replied Omar, not bullied by Saeed's words or attitude.

CHAPTER FIVE
Middle Eastern Promise

They flew out late that afternoon on an Air France flight to Dubai. On arrival, they encountered a problem. It was no problem for the girls to enter Dubai on a visit visa, but Masood and Ali were Indian Nationals and had no such automatic right of entry. After an hour at immigration, Masood persuaded the official to allow him to make a phone call. Within minutes, they were ushered through and on the way to The Hilton.

"Who the hell did you call Masood, the King?" demanded Cindy. Masood laughed.

"Not quite my love, but close, and they don't have Kings here they are called Sheiks."

"I don't care who it was," said Mel. "I'm impressed." Ali wasn't impressed. It just added to his worries that their presence in Dubai was known.

"It's hot here," said Cindy.

"Yes, and it will be even hotter when the sun comes up tomorrow morning. At least it will be cool in our hotel and we don't have to leave there if we don't want."

The hotel, as with most others in Dubai, was magnificent, with cool marble everywhere and staff who knew what the word service meant. There can be little doubt that a stay in any of the top hotels in Dubai is special and Mel and Cindy were in for a time to remember.

After the excitement at the airport, they all slept remarkably well and woke up to bright sunshine. It was already 30 degrees outside, but the air conditioning belied the outside heat. Down in the restaurant, was a buffet style breakfast fit for any Sheik, and they ate heartily.

"What would you like to do ladies?" asked Ali.

"I want to visit the market, but here I think they call it a Souk," said Cindy.

"Yes," agreed Masood. "May I suggest we go later when it has cooled down?" They spent the rest of the day lazing by the pool, sipping drinks and eating snacks. The sun beat down, but it felt cool under the large coloured umbrellas and regular dips in the pool, even though the water was warm, cooled them nicely.

"Why are those men watching us?" asked Mel. "I'm sure the big one is the man who hit George."

"Yes he is," Cindy agreed.

"It is nothing to worry about honestly," replied Masood. "They're here for our protection."

"Why do we need protecting and from who?" asked Mel.

"No one in particular, but we are wealthy men and you can't be too careful these days," Masood answered.

That evening they went to the Souk, and wandered through the tiny back streets of Dubai old town, with its mud buildings and dusty streets. It was busy and the traders recognized them as tourists with that sixth sense only an Arab market trader has. They tried to entice them with carpets and cloth, watches and brass goods, until they walked around a corner and found a most amazing scene, a street lined with shops selling gold. Masood and Ali had known it was around here somewhere, but had wanted the fun of letting the girls find it.

Their faces were a picture and Ali wished he had a camera.

"My God is it real?" gasped Cindy. The amazement was written across her face for all to see.

"Yes, it's all the real thing and not nine carat either. If you ask them for nine carat they will be insulted."

The gold was so shiny it did not seem real and the ornate designs were fantastic. The shops were busy with more Arab women around than any other nationality. They argued and bargained with the shopkeepers in Arabic at a pace which made Mel wonder how they had time for breath, and sometimes the bargaining was so loud that she thought any second a fight would break out. Amazingly, it always seemed to end in smiles all around and an excited exit from the shop wearing the trophy.

"Aren't they worried they may get mugged or robbed on the way home?" asked Mel of one of the shopkeepers.

"No, we have little crime here because it is not worth the risk. They cut your hand and foot off for stealing here madam," he smiled.

"Ugh!" was Mel's reaction. "Barbaric."

"You may think so madam, but it works. You can walk around here wearing as much gold as you can carry and no one will touch you."

Cindy had spotted a bracelet she liked and the shopkeeper sensed her vulnerability in a flash.

"Madam likes the bracelet. It is very beautiful just like her." He had it on her wrist in a flash.

"See how it sparkles," he said settling into a sales pitch older than he was. He knew the sale was made as soon as she allowed him to put it on her wrist.

"What do you think Masood?" she asked with a sparkle in her eye only matched by the gold on her wrist.

"It is nearly as beautiful as you my love."

"Flattery will get you everywhere," she smiled.

"I will have it."

"Not so quick my love, you're supposed to haggle the price with him," laughed Masood.

"Oh I forgot," she said embarrassed.

"I will give you last price anyway madam. That will be two thousand five hundred Dirhams madam."

"How much is that in real money?" she asked.

"You are English, yes?" he asked.

"Yes." He got out his calculator and came up with "420 sterling pounds madam."

"God that's cheap Mel," said Cindy.

"I can make it more if madam wishes," joked the shopkeeper, knowing they were now going to buy more than one bracelet.

"You take these?" she said producing a credit card from her purse.

"Sorry madam cash or American Express."

"What about traveller's cheques?" asked Cindy.

"Those will do nicely madam."

Before they left the shop, Mel had bought a necklace, and Masood and Ali had ordered the girls' names in Arabic which they could collect two days later. Mel looked a bit odd wearing her necklace over her t-shirt but she was too proud of it to care. They continued wandering around the gold Souk with the girls eyeing up everything in every shop, until the shops began to close.

"Don't worry we will be back before we leave Dubai, Ali and I have some gifts to buy," assured Masood. "And now we must eat." They got a taxi to the newer part of town and went into a roadside café.

"We're not eating here are we?" asked Mel wrinkling up her nose.

"Yes," replied Masood. "This is the best curry house in Dubai."

Not sure, the girls looked over the menu several times.

"Have you decided ladies?" asked Masood, with a grin all over his face.

"No," they replied. "What are you having?"

"Well, there is only one dish to have here and that's the Chicken Butter Boneless. Would you like to try it?"

"Why not," they agreed. Ali ordered for them all in Hindi, which took the girls a bit by surprise. The food was not long in coming and arrived piping hot. By now, the girls were hungry and tucked in straight away.

"This is delicious Masood," exclaimed Cindy, followed by an agreeing nod from Mel.

"Yes, it is my cousin's speciality."

"Your cousin works here?" asked an amazed Cindy.

"No my dear, he owns the place," replied Masood laughing.

"He should open a place in London. This would go down a bomb, he would make a fortune," replied Cindy.

"He has tried, but he can't get a visa. He was a bit naughty when he was young and you British are funny about things like that," laughed Masood.

The dish was not hot in the usual curry way, but very tasty. It was made up of strips of chicken in a mild dark sauce.

"Can I get the recipe before we leave?" Cindy asked.

"Sorry Cindy," piped up Masood. "He won't tell anyone. It's a family secret and I have never found it anywhere before, not even in India." As if on cue, his cousin appeared.

"Is it to your liking ladies?"

"It's fantastic," answered Cindy, flashing the man a huge smile of approval.

"Thank you kindly, your praise is very kind."

"Masood says you will not give me the recipe," she said.

"He is right. Many people have asked me, but I never tell."

"Oh well, it was worth asking. It really is delicious," said Cindy, disappointment clearly in her voice. They chatted for a while then got a taxi back to the hotel and retired for the night.

The next day, Masood suggested they go on a safari out into the desert. Everyone agreed and an hour after breakfast their jeep turned up to collect them. It was hot and they were grateful that the jeep had air conditioning. The driver headed out of Dubai, on the road to Abu Dhabi and turned off into the desert just after passing Jebel Ali.

"That's the largest man-made port in the world," the driver told them. "It has been cut out of the sand and made up of massive concrete blocks. Sheik Rashid had it built."

He drove up a long sand dune so they could get a better look. The heat caused the sand to shimmer and look as if it was moving. Then after a brief pause, they were off down the other side and off into the true desert. It was not long before they came across a group of camels and a family of Bedouins.

"Can we stop?" asked Mel.

"Yes," said the driver. "But if they don't come over to the jeep we must move on."

"Why?" she asked.

"They can be very funny and sometimes dangerous. You must let them make the first move and whatever you do, don't go near their tents," the driver warned.

An old man approached the jeep and spoke to the driver in guttural Arabic. The driver continued the conversation, clearly fluent in the language.

"We have been invited to take coffee with them. It is a great honour, but there are rules. The coffee is very strong but you must drink it. If they offer a refill and you don't want any more, simply hold your hand palm down over your cup. Most importantly, do not stare at any of the women."

He was right, the coffee was very thick and sweet, and clearly an acquired taste. Cindy was fascinated by the camels and could not resist leaving the group to go and look at them. She bent down to get a closer look at one, when the driver grabbed her hand and dragged her away. The Bedouin men laughed and she got embarrassed.

"Why did you do that?" she snapped, pulling her arm free and glaring at the confused driver.

"He was about to spit in your face and it has been known to cause blindness," he replied, obviously offended that his help was not appreciated.

"I am sorry," she apologized, even more embarrassed now. "I did not realise they were so dangerous."

"We should go now," the driver announced. He thanked the elder for the hospitality, and they left. Cindy was silent for the next part of the journey. She had been shaken by the incident with the camel and was still embarrassed as well. They stopped in a hollow between two sand dunes and Mel started to get out.

"No madam please, do not get out, just sit and watch," urged the driver.

They sat in silence for what seemed like ages and with no engine running there was no air conditioning. It was uncomfortable and Ali was just about to speak when about ten feet in front of the jeep a large flying black beetle landed, then another and then more. Soon there were about twenty of them spread around the hollow.

"Watch carefully," whispered the driver.

Without warning, the sand erupted near one of the beetles and a scorpion dashed the short distance, grabbed the bewildered beetle in its claws, and stung it. The end was swift, but then there were other eruptions and the same happened again and again. The scorpions, along with their prey, vanished into the sand as quickly as they had arrived.

"That's amazing," said Mel. "How did you know that was going to happen?"

"It's my job madam," replied the driver.

"And if we had gotten out, would they have attacked us?" asked Mel.

"Yes madam, they sense the vibration and attack on instinct. One alone is not enough to kill, but it would make you very sick. More than one may be enough to kill you, it depends how strong you are."

"Thank you for stopping me from getting out," stuttered a shaken Mel.

Their return to the hotel was uneventful. They had a quiet dinner that evening in the hotel and retired early. Ali was in need of some tender loving care and Mel was more than happy to provide it.

CHAPTER SIX
Death Lurks Below

"I have an adventure planned for tomorrow," Ali told Mel as they cuddled in the large bed.

"What is it?" she asked.

"I'm not telling. It's a secret, but I am sure you will all like it."

Morning came and Ali was up early buzzing around the suite like an excited schoolboy, making and receiving calls. Each call was treated as if he was a secret agent. They had breakfast in the suite and at 11:00 am, Ali received a call from reception to tell him their car had arrived.

"Quick we have no time to waste," he said urging them all through the door like an eager sheepdog.

A white stretched limousine awaited them at the door with the rear door being held open by a smartly dressed Indian driver.

"Now that's style Ali," said Mel. At those words, Ali seemed to grow taller and a big beaming smile spread across his face. He helped Mel and Cindy in following them quickly into the cavernous luxurious interior. The red carpet in the car was thick and felt like walking on air and there was a distinctive smell of leather which hit them as they stepped inside. The seats were deep and sumptuous and the heavily tinted windows blocked out the glare of the sun.

"This is wonderful, where are we going?" asked Mel.

"To Mina Seheeya for a picnic and a day of relaxing and swimming in the sea," he announced.

On arrival, they got out and were met by the sight of a man-made lagoon. It was made from rocks which went out into the sea from the left in the shape of a C with the end cut off. From the right, more rocks went out into the sea forming the cut-off end of the C. They did not meet, but left a gap about forty metres wide through which the sea entered.

"This is beautiful Ali," gasped Mel, as she emerged from the cool interior of the limo.

"Yes, a friend told me if I ever came to Dubai, I must come here," said Ali.

It was deserted except for them. While they were talking, the driver had set up a large square umbrella and under it a table on which he had set tall champagne flutes of the finest crystal. They sparkled and shone reflecting the dazzling sunlight.

"Shall I open the champagne now Sir?" he asked Ali.

"Yes please," Ali replied.

"You mentioned swimming Ali, but we have no costumes. Are we going in naked?" asked Cindy.

"No. We would get arrested if the police came. You will find a choice of costumes in the small case which I took to the car with me, and you can get changed in the car. The darkened windows will protect your modesty," chuckled Ali.

Off went Cindy and Mel who spent ages changing, but this at least gave Ali and Masood time for a bit of man talk.

"So, are you enjoying Dubai or are you still worried that they will come and get us at any moment and whisk us away to their torture chambers," joked Masood.

"It's not funny Masood. I think you are right, but when I see those men following us around it makes my blood run cold. I dread to think what they would do to my Mel."

"I am sure we are safe or I would not have brought us here in the first place my friend," said Masood. He could not know how wrong he was to be proved before the day was over.

The girls finally emerged from the car and it was worth the wait. Mel had chosen a high cut yellow one-piece making her legs look even longer than usual. Straps joined at the back of her neck allowing all of her back to be on show. The material clung tightly and the colour accentuated her tan even more. Ali could not take his eyes off her. He had seen her undressed and that was sexy, but in this costume she was a goddess. The costume was tight and just about covered her pubic region. The material was stretched tight over her taught stomach before curving out and straining to capture and hold her ample breasts.

"Wow!" was Ali's only word.

Cindy had chosen a red and black bikini. The lower half was only a thong and the top half just large enough to hold her breasts but small enough to hold any man's attention. Masood was thrilled. He too loved Cindy naked, but he also liked a little mystery.

"Come on gents, your turn," said Mel and Cindy together. Ali and Masood just dropped their pants and grinned.

"That's cheating, you were already changed," protested Mel.

The grins just got bigger and they all burst out laughing.

"The champagne is getting warm," announced Ali leading them to the umbrella-covered table and tripping over a small rock while his eyes stayed glued to Mel. This caused another round of raucous laughter which was interrupted by the sound of a large speedboat coming into the lagoon.

"Wouldn't you know it," moaned Cindy. "We were just going to have the perfect day and some bastard spoils our privacy."

The boat headed towards the shore where they were standing and she turned to see Ali and Masood trying to stifle laughter.

"Ok you guy's what's the joke?" she demanded.

"The boat's for us," Masood said as he got out, before nearly choking on his own laughter and the champagne he was trying to swallow.

"God! You are in for it later Masood," joked Cindy.

"Is that a threat or a promise Cindy?" laughed Masood. He knew exactly what she meant and that made the day even better.

They were soon on the boat heading out into the blue waters of the Gulf. The breeze caused by the forward speed of the boat as it bucked and tossed its way through the water was very cooling. They sat on deep leather seats of pale blue on the aft deck with Masood trying to pour the wine while the boat rolled and bucked across the waves.

"This is the life eh Cindy," Mel joked.

"Yes, and it can be like this forever my love if you wish it," said Ali.

"Does that go for me as well?" asked Cindy to no one in particular.

"If you like," replied Masood casually.

"You're really in for it when we get back to the hotel Masood," she threatened.

"Promises, promises," laughed Masood.

They returned to the beach about two hours later for a late lunch of a barbeque which the driver had just finished preparing when they arrived. The food smelled good and the sea breeze had given them all an appetite. They wolfed down the food which was helped down with cold champagne from the fridge in the limo.

"That was great. Now who's for a swim?" asked Ali running for the water. Mel was right behind him as they swam out to the middle of the lagoon and were swimming around and playing.

"Ouch," said Ali. "I've just been bitten."

"Was it a fish?" asked Mel.

"Don't know," replied Ali staring hard into the water. Keeping still they looked in the settling water for any sign of a fish but there were none around. They swam for the shore and Ali stumbled onto the beach.

"What's wrong?" shouted Masood.

"Ali has been bitten," shouted back Mel.

Cindy, Masood and the driver rushed to see what was wrong. They looked at Ali's ankle and there were four tiny wounds.

"Oh mother of God!! It is a sea snake bite and they can be deadly. We have to get him to the hospital quickly," urged the driver. Masood picked up Ali like a child. He was already looking very sickly. His skin was greying and cold to the touch as they rushed to the limo.

"Go! Just go," shouted Masood at the panicked driver.

"Don't worry about what we've left behind I will cover the cost, if my friend dies I will kill you anyway," threatened Masood.

Mel sat at the far end of a long seat and Ali was laid along the seat with his head on her lap as they sped back to Dubai.

"Do you have a phone or radio in the car?" Masood asked. The driver nodded and passed Masood a handset. He dialed a number.

"I am Masood Jaleel and I want a police escort now," he roared down the phone then gave the handset to the driver.

"Tell them where we are," he shouted.

The terrified driver screamed their location into the handset. It was only minutes, but it seemed like forever. Soon the car was bracketed by three speeding police cars, with sirens wailing and blue lights flashing. They roared along the road like four racing cars, dust from the side of the road choking the air, and blinding all the cars and trucks as they passed. Traffic at roundabouts had been stopped to clear their passage.

"Shit! Look at his leg," screeched Cindy clasping her hands to her already drained face.

Ali's leg was swelling as they watched. How could skin stretch like that she thought. It was already three times its normal size and still swelling. Thankfully, Ali had passed out with the pain. Mel looked down at his face on her lap and in that moment, knew the answer to Ali's question. She loved this little man and although she had never prayed in her life before, she silently prayed now.

The limo was not built for this sort of driving and the journey was a rough ride but they got to Rashid Hospital where emergency staff waited. Ali was rushed to a special suite kept only for poison bite or sting victims. Masood, Mel and Cindy waited for what seemed like an eternity; then a doctor came.

"It is a snake bite of that we are sure. Did you capture the snake?" he asked.

"Are you fucking mad? We were in the water and couldn't see anything, and even if we had, we weren't going to try to catch something that can do this," exploded Mel.

"Please do not swear and please calm down. I have to ask these questions. If we know which type of snake it was, we can treat your friend quicker and with the right anti venom. If not, then we have to wait," said the doctor, trying to calm the situation.

"Wait! Wait for what?" blurted out Mel hysterically.

"We know the fangs punctured the skin, but we do not know how much poison it injected, if any. So we have to do constant blood tests to see if we can identify the poison and if the blood is thickening."

"I don't understand what you are saying. Will Ali live or not?" demanded Cindy.

"It is hard to say," replied the besieged doctor. Just then another doctor came and spoke to the first doctor.

"I have some good news. We at least know the poison type now, so we know which anti venom to give to your friend."

"So he will be fine," smiled Mel weakly.

"I did not say that. We have to wait and see if his blood thickens. You see, snake venom causes the blood to thicken until the heart can no longer pump it around the body. Anti venom thins the blood down. If we give it to your friend before we are sure, we could kill him by thinning his blood and it will boil in his body," replied the doctor.

"Oh God what a choice," Mel gasped, before collapsing onto the floor. She awoke on a bed to see the smiling faces of Cindy and Masood.

"Ali?" asked Mel.

"Yes my dear, he will be fine," comforted Masood, patting her hand gently.

"A tough sod that man of yours," added Cindy.

"What do you mean that man of mine?" asked Mel.

"You know damn well what I mean. I saw the look on your face when we were coming here and we've known each other too long for you to fool me girl," replied Cindy.

"Ok I admit it, I love him," said Mel.

"Thank God for that, now go and tell him," said Masood.

"You can leave here tomorrow as long as you rest Mr Beg," assured the doctor. "The swelling will go down quickly, but you must drink plenty of water to help flush the toxins out of your system. You're a very lucky man."

"Yes doctor I am," smiled Ali, holding Mel's hand so tight she thought he would crush it. She stayed with him until he fell asleep and only went then because the nurses promised he would be safe and was in no danger.

Returning to the hotel, Mel went up to the suite and talked with Masood and Cindy for a while before turning in. She cried a lot that night, not tears of sadness but of relief. She had thought during that nightmare journey to the hospital that she would lose him and knew it would have broken her heart.

How, she asked herself that night, could she feel the way she did for a man who she did not even know two weeks ago. He was not handsome or tall or strong, but he had the sort of kindness she had never known before, like he had shown on the first night in the incident with George. He was as quick as a whip and as brave as a lion. He was as passionate as other lovers had been, but in their gentle moments she thought he would melt her like warm chocolate. He did things to her body she did not know were possible.

If truth be told, she had been impressed by his wealth at first, but that did not matter anymore. Her life was now richer than any money could buy.

Cindy came to her in the night and they talked for a while as she poured her heart out and felt the better for it.

"You have got it bad love, but you could do worse," assured Cindy.

"What about you and Masood?" Mel asked.

"We're ok love, honest. He suits me and I think I suit him, but we will see as time goes by," confided Cindy.

Cindy left her to her thoughts. Mel slept fitfully, waking frequently with a start to find he wasn't beside her. She rang the hospital at about 2:00 am but they said he was fine and they were sure he could leave that afternoon. She ached to hold him in her arms and tell him she loved him, but knew she had to wait.

On her return to their bedroom, Cindy found Masood sat up in bed smiling.

"What are you looking so pleased about?" Cindy asked.

"Well, before Ali was bitten you made some promises, or were they threats? asked Masood, smiling.

"I'll save them for another time lover. I don't feel in the mood right now," Cindy replied.

He was disappointed, but knew she was right. He wasn't sure how he felt either. It had been a close call with Ali and he knew it. Even he did not know how close to disaster their plans had come. He had taken care of the limo driver who could not believe the size of the cheque Masood had given him. The tip could have bought a new limo.

They all went to the hospital in the same limo to collect Ali and he had his chance to thank the driver personally, when he could speak in between Mel kissing him.

"Careful woman, you will break me in two," joked Ali.

"Then I will have two of you," Mel retorted.

The swelling on his leg had reduced to nearly normal, but was still painful as was his manhood where they had removed the catheter. They had pumped as much fluid into him on a drip as they could to help clear the toxins out of his system. A catheter was used, as they did not want him getting out of bed for the toilet every ten minutes.

"Is it too sore to work," joked Mel. "Or does it need kissing better?"

"Lots of kissing better," he joked. "It's not up to anything else," he laughed.

"That's a first then," Mel retorted.

"Don't you two ever think of anything else?" joined Cindy. "Why? Is there anything else," laughed Ali and Mel together.

"They're even thinking the same now Masood," said Cindy.

"Yes, there is no hope for them now. They must be in love. They will be ending each other's sentences next," replied Masood.

He laughed and they all joined in. Even Ahmed the driver was laughing. The journey from Rashid Hospital to the hotel was thankfully a short one. Ali was glad to get into the hotel suite and went straight to bed accompanied by Mel, who administered plenty of tender loving care before he fell into a deep, but troubled sleep. She did not leave him, but cuddled as close as she could, eventually falling asleep herself.

When he awoke, Ali found her asleep next to him. She had clearly been crying a lot before falling asleep. He looked at her in wonder, not sure why such a wonderful beautiful woman like Mel had fallen in love with him, but he was happier than he had ever been that she had.

"Come on you sleepy heads," said Masood. He entered the bedroom without knocking and interrupted Ali's loving thought, and startling Mel from her slumber. She woke up with a start and instinctively reached for where Ali had lain. He was smiling as he reached for her and she buried her head on his hairless chest and sobbed.

"I am fine darling. Everything is fine, please don't cry," said Ali.

Meanwhile, Masood was backing out of the door, red faced with embarrassment.

Mel held Ali tight for a long while, not willing to risk him being out of her reach again after so nearly losing him forever.

Eventually they got up, showered and dressed, while Masood ordered dinner in the suite.

They went to the Souk that evening to collect the name necklaces and the girls were thrilled. They wore them on the way back to the hotel as if they were wearing the most precious diamonds in the world. Having dined in the hotel, they went up to the suite, as Ali's leg was sore and he wanted to retire. He and Mel left the others in the lounge and went to bed. She held him that night and told him what he wanted to hear. He was halfway out of bed on the way to tell Masood and Cindy when she pulled him back.

"No need my love, they know," Mel whispered.

"But how do they know?" asked Ali.

"They guessed when we were in the car on the way to the hospital; I was so afraid I was going to lose you," said Mel.

He was upset that he was not the first to know, but he could not be angry with her or let it show. They cuddled close that night and her closeness seemed to ease the pain.

She woke up to find him gone. He was gone some time and when he returned, he did not seem himself. When she spoke to him he did not answer, but she cuddled up to him and they were both soon asleep.

"Where did you go to last night Ali?" asked Mel while they were getting ready for breakfast.

"I did not go anywhere my love," replied Ali.

"But you left the room for a while about 2:30 this morning," said Mel.

"Did I? I don't remember. Did I disturb you? If so, I'm sorry," Ali apologized.

"Don't worry about that. I was just worried in case it was anything to do with your leg hurting you," said Mel.

"No my love, I don't think so. But I don't remember going anywhere," said Ali, confused.

"Let's forget it. It's not important. What are we doing today?" asked Mel.

"I don't know. Maybe Masood has some suggestions," replied Ali.

CHAPTER SEVEN
Home from Home

The phone rang in Saeed's suite causing him to jump up quickly.

"Yes," snapped Saeed into the receiver.

"We have the letter you asked for," said the desk clerk to Captain Saeed.

"Don't send it up to the room. Someone will collect it," said Saeed. Khalaf was there in two minutes and returned with the letter to Saeed.

"Good now we shall see what it says and then arrest these dogs," said Saeed. He carefully opened the letter and read the contents. He was baffled that the only information on the sheet of paper was the name of the next hotel, the city and a flight number.

"What good is this?" Saeed ranted. "It tells us nothing of use. There are no codes or frequencies. Nothing of any use. Get that fool of a clerk and bring him here. He has given us the wrong letter and will pay dearly."

The clerk was trembling when he entered Saeed's suite.

"What is this rubbish?" Saeed demanded. "Where is the other letter?"

"There is no other letter," the clerk replied. A spreading stain in his groin area showed how frightened he was.

"There must be," demanded Saeed.

"Honestly, I have checked and there are no other letters for this man or his friend," pleaded the clerk.

"Get out of my sight," growled Saeed. "If I find out you are lying, you and your family will die very slowly."

The clerk ran from the room with pee running from the bottom of his trouser leg.

"Stop," shouted Khalaf.

The petrified clerk froze in his tracks, wondering what was going to happen, but too afraid to turn around.

"Come back," Khalaf summoned.

Shaking from head to toe, the clerk obeyed.

"You still need to deliver this you idiot," roared Saeed. He thrust the letter into the terrified clerk's hand. "Now go. Do not let me see your ugly face again."

Masood collected the letter from reception ten minutes later. He was unaware that it had been opened. He read the contents and returned to the suite.

"It is time to pack," announced Masood.

"Where to this time?" asked Ali.

"Bombay. We are going home for a few days," replied Masood, beaming.

"Fantastic. Bloody fantastic," shouted Cindy. "Can we go to the Taj Mahal. I have always wanted to go there. Please Masood. Please say we can."

"Of course we can. If you want to go there my love, we can do whatever you want. It may sound strange, as it is such an important place in our country, but Ali and I have never been there either," said Masood.

"You're pulling our legs. You must have been there," said Cindy.

"No my love, I am serious," promised Masood.

So please pack. I have a phone call to make," announced Masood, rising and leaving the suite.

Ali was as excited as the girls. He would have the chance to show Mel the sights of Bombay and Delhi and he was getting out of Dubai. It was a nervous time as they packed and went to the airport. He felt jittery until they were on the plane and in the air.

"What is wrong Ali?" asked Mel. "Is your leg bothering you? You seem very nervous."

"It's nothing my love, honest," replied Ali, glancing around the airport terminal for the thousandth time.

When they were going through immigration, he thought he was going to wet himself as the passport officer looked at his passport, then back to

Ali, then back to the passport. It took all his control to stop his hand shaking as he took his passport from the officer's hand.

"I hope you have enjoyed your stay," said the man. Ali smiled weakly back and muttered unconvincingly that he had.

The time spent in the departure lounge was an hour. But to Ali, it felt like a lifetime and by the time they boarded the plane, he was feeling very ill.

"What is wrong Ali? Shall we get off and take you to hospital?" asked Mel.

"No! No, I will be fine. It must be something I ate last night," pleaded Ali. "There is no need to get off."

"But your face is grey and you're sweating a lot," replied Mel.

"Please, just let me sleep I will be fine in a while, honestly," assured Ali. He settled into the large comfortable first class seat and looking around the cabin at his fellow travellers he finally felt safe and closed his eyes. By the time they had been in the air half an hour, he was feeling much better and looking full of life.

"Would you like something to drink Sir?" asked the stewardess.

"Yes please," replied Ali. "I will have champagne."

"That's more like my Ali," chirped Mel. "I was worried about you at the airport you looked so ill."

"Yes I felt it too my love, but I feel so much better now. Perhaps it was the last of the poison going through my system," replied Ali.

Nice one Ali thought Masood. You're a better liar than I thought you were.

By the time the plane landed in Bombay, Ali was well drunk and harangued the customs and immigration staff as they passed through them.

"They are just doing their job. Don't be so rude," pleaded Mel. Meanwhile Masood smoothed the officials' ruffled feathers with a few well placed bribes.

Once in the suite at the hotel, Mel let it fly.

"Ali, what is wrong with you? Your behaviour at the airport was disgraceful and I was so embarrassed," Mel ranted.

"Yes, and that goes for me too," joined in Cindy.

"Shut up, Cindy. This is my row and I'll thank you to keep your nose out," snapped Mel. She grabbed a sullen Ali's hand and dragged him off to the bedroom. She slammed the door, but she could still be heard chewing Ali to bits inside.

Masood kept quiet. He knew when to speak and when not to, and now was a time for silence. It went quiet after about an hour and then Mel emerged with a very embarrassed Ali, who apologized.

"It's time to eat," said Masood breaking the tension in the room. This hotel has some of the finest Indian food in the world.

At dinner, Ali was quiet and ate little. He still felt like a naughty boy and wanted to go back to the suite to make up with Mel.

After dinner, they retired and she saw a different Ali that night as he tried to make up for his bad behaviour. He wished he could explain to her why he had behaved the way he did, but he dare not. One day maybe, but not yet.

Breakfast saw smiles on everyone's faces as Masood announced they were going to fly to Delhi, and then travel on to Agra to see the Taj Mahal.

The flight to Delhi was not as good as the flight from Dubai. There was no first class section and the plane was old. It sounded like it would fall apart at any time, but it had made the flight many times before and held together this time as well. The trip to the hotel from the airport was full of wonder for Mel and Cindy.

"What are all these cows doing in the road and why does the traffic take such care to go around them?" asked Mel.

"They are sacred cows and anyone hitting them would have a crowd around him instantly, and be beaten to death."

"Don't wind me up Ali," pleaded Mel.

"He is not. What Ali says is true. In the Hindu religion, the cow is sacred and must not be touched or hurt," explained Masood. "And if you hit them because they wander into you or your car and it's an accident… then it's the last accident you will ever have my dear, the crowd will make sure of that," continued Masood.

"But won't the police help?" asked Mel.

"No, but if they did, they would be killed too," advised Masood.

"Why is it that at every traffic light there are lots of boys and girls with deformed limbs waiting around?" asked Cindy.

"They are professional beggars and as soon as they see non-Indian people in a car and it stops at a junction, they surround it. We are stopping at these lights. See what happens when the lights change," said Masood.

The taxi drew to a halt and was instantly surrounded by the beggars. When the lights changed, the driver honked his horn but no one moved and they were trapped.

"What now?" asked Cindy.

Masood wound down the taxi window and threw some coins as far as he could. They had hardly left his hand before the beggars were off after them.

"How do they move so fast with their legs and arms twisted at those angles?" asked Cindy.

"Many years of practice my dear," replied Masood.

"But how do they get like that? Are they born disfigured?" asked Cindy.

"Some are. Most are made that way by their parents who break their bones and tie them up when they are small children so that they will be pitiful later in life; and people like you will feel sorry for them and give them lots of money," explained Masood.

"Ugh. How disgusting, and cruel," said Mel, frowning and pulling several horrible faces in rapid succession.

"It is a cruel world out here and many nasty things have to be done to survive," replied Masood.

Delhi has an ugly side and a beautiful side. As they reached the grounds of the Royal Raj Hotel, they were met by opulence beyond imagination. Once through the guarded gates, the grounds were lush with tall palm trees gently blowing in the wind, and lush rolling green lawns. The hotel building was painted a pale blue, adorned with golden domes, and looked like something out of an old film set.

The doormen were in magnificent costumes of blue baggy pantaloons held up by a broad gold cummerbund, then a cream loose shirt, and a blue and gold waistcoat. All of this was finished off with a gold turban.

Inside, the hotel was cool, yet light and airy with more palm trees and plants in the main lobby and a central fountain.

They quickly checked in and went to their suite, which continued the magnificence of the rest of the hotel. On the table awaiting them, was a silver bucket of ice, with a bottle of Bollinger nestling in the ice, fresh fruit, and lots of flowers. The scent from the multitude of flowers arranged around the room was overwhelming.

"This is fantastic. What a beautiful place, but I can't get those beggars in the city out of my mind," said Mel.

"It is the way life is in India. The rich are very rich, and the poor are very poor, and you worrying about it won't change a thing. If it will make you feel better, we can go out later and give them some money, but you must promise me that whatever you see you will not try to get out of the car," said Ali.

"I promise Ali, I promise," replied Mel.

"That goes for me as well," butted in Cindy.

"In that case, I will go and organize some money," promised Masood.

While Masood was doing this, Cindy started to unpack. Mel and Ali went for a walk around the magnificent grounds.

"I can't believe we are here. It's like a dream," said Mel.

"Yes my love, I sometimes have to pinch myself as well," confided Ali.

"But you are rich. You must be used to this," said Mel.

"I am now, but it has not always been that way. I have known times when I was hungry enough to eat other people's leftovers," said Ali.

"Ugh! Ali that is awful."

"Yes, but it makes you appreciate when you are well off. I have no intention of ever going back there again," replied Ali.

They walked hand in hand around the beautiful gardens in silence for a while, each lost in their own private thoughts.

The gardens were truly fantastic with a wide variety of trees, bushes, rolling lawns and magnificent sculptures. They reached the top of some steps leading down to a pool with a fountain, where the water spurted from a myriad of animals' mouths onto a central column rising about sixty feet into the air, topped by a golden statue of a sacred cow.

"Shall we go down and look closer?" asked Mel.

"My leg is sore my love, would you mind if we didn't. Maybe another day," replied Ali.

"Of course not Ali, I was not thinking," Mel replied.

They continued along the path for about fifty metres then, without warning, a man stepped from behind a palm tree and pointed a dagger at Mel.

"Give me your money and I will not harm her," he threatened.

Taken by surprise, Mel stood rooted to the spot, too terrified to move. Ali reached slowly into his jacket for his wallet. He would gladly give all he had in the world to save Mel from harm. As Ali stretched out his hand to give the man his wallet, the man clutched his neck. In slow motion, he fell to the ground. On hitting the ground, his hand fell away to reveal a small dart sticking out of his neck. As if by magic, hotel staff appeared and ushered Ali and Mel away. Others came and collected the fallen man and placed his body in a cart. Within minutes, the scene looked as if nothing had ever happened.

Ali and Mel were shown to their suite by a very embarrassed manager.

"I am so sorry for this Sir, Madam. This is the first time we have had this happen for many years," explained the manager.

"Who was he and where did he come from?" asked Ali.

"We do not know who he was but he had cut through the fence near where he tried to take your wallet," the manager continued.

"He will be dealt with by the police?" demanded Ali.

"It is too late for that Sir. He is beyond questioning," explained the manager.

"Why?"

"He is dead Sir! We have many important guests staying here at all times and we cannot take any chances. Some years ago, we installed a special security system. If our fence is cut or we detect an intruder, we send out our removal team who are armed with darts and blowpipe. They are all experienced hunters and they track and eliminate the problem," said the manager.

"Problem, bloody problem!" exploded a shaken Mel. "You make him sound like an animal."

"Pardon me Madam, but these people are a danger to our guests. We must do what we see fit to protect the people who have entrusted us with their safety. If it has upset you, I am sorry, but we can take no chances. They feel no pain and death is instant," he explained.

Urghhhhhhh. Mel's vomit went everywhere and even the poor manager got a share, before she fled the room.

Ali knew the manager was right and waved him to leave so he could talk to a now sobbing Mel. While they talked in their bedroom, two cleaners came and cleared up the mess, while the confused manager explained to Masood and Cindy what had happened.

Ali and Mel did not join Masood and Cindy for dinner that night, but stayed in their bedroom talking long into the night. Ali tried to explain to Mel the value of life in India, or rather the lack of value placed on a life.

CHAPTER EIGHT
Beauty and the Beast

After breakfast the next morning, they left for Agra by car. The mood was sombre at first, until they stopped at a roadside café which had elephants nearby. Both the girls were fascinated by them because they were huge, and also, because they were free. They had only seen them in a circus before and behind bars at the zoo.

"Would you like to ride one Mel?" asked Ali, hoping to lighten her mood.

"I would love to. Do you think they would let me?" giggled Mel.

"I will see what I can do," said Ali, scampering off to speak to the mahout.

"And me," shouted Cindy after Ali.

Ali returned in a few minutes and ushered them to the waiting elephants.

"Oh, I'm not sure," said Mel. "Now that I'm next to them, they seem so huge."

"True madam," said the mahout. "But they are gentle giants and will not hurt you at all."

"How do I get on?" asked Mel, only to feel a trunk gently squeezing her waist and lifting her into the air. Shrieking she was placed gently on the enormous back and the trunk slid from her waist. She watched in wonder as another elephant did the same to Cindy. Then they were off down a track swaying gently back and forth with the movement of the elephants.

The ride lasted about half an hour during which the girls constantly giggled and pointed at each other. Meanwhile, Ali was busy taking pictures from every angle. Masood did a video recording of the spectacle. Then, they were off on the road to Agra.

On arriving, they were amazed at the number of people in the grounds of the Taj Mahal, a true wonder of the world. A guide quickly attached himself to them and took them around the gardens and building, pointing out its many fascinating facets.

He stopped at a corner of the building. "…And now ladies and gentlemen if you look up and down at the marble, and the pattern inset in black on the white marble, you will notice that the pattern at the top looks the same size as the pattern at the bottom."

It was true it did.

"But how is that possible?" asked Cindy.

"I do not know the details Madam, but they were very clever craftsmen in those days, and believe me it does not matter where you look at the Taj from, the pattern always appears the same size," assured the guide.

He took them inside the mausoleum where they had to cover their noses because the stench of guano is so strong. He told them that the Taj had been built by Shah Jahan for his beloved wife, Mumtaz Mahal, as her final resting place.

"Shah Jahan was the fifth son of Emperor Jahangir, who ruled in the 16th century what we now know as India. Such was the courage and ability of the then young Prince Khurram that his father granted him the title 'Shah Jahan', 'King of the World'. A tribute never before paid to an uncrowned Mughal King," continued the guide.

"When Jahangir's health started to fail, his sons rivaled for succession to his throne. After years of battle and the deaths of his brothers, under suspicious circumstances in 1628, Shah Jahan ascended to the throne. In 1631 Shah Jahan set out with his armies to subdue a rebellion in Barhanpur, accompanied by his wife Mumtaz. She died after giving birth to their fourteenth child, and it is said with her dying breath she secured a promise from Shah Jahan to build her the most beautiful mausoleum the world had ever seen. Six months after her death, he laid the foundations for the Taj Mahal which took twenty two years and twenty thousand men to build."

"He found solace on his visits to her tomb, with his children, but not for long. Just as he had conspired against his brothers for his father, Jahangir's, empire, so his son Aurangzeb assailed Shah Jahan's throne, and in

1658 Aurangzeb declared himself Emperor and imprisoned his father in the Red Fort in Agra."

"If you follow me, I will show you where his mausoleum was going to be."

They left the building to go out into the bright sunshine, and after a few minutes, their eyes became accustomed to the bright light.

"If you look across the river you will see the foundations of another Taj. This is as far as it ever got," explained the guide.

"Why?" jumped in Cindy.

"It is a sad tale Madam, but he intended to build a copy of this one in black marble, with the same pattern in white. Before he could do that, he was deposed by his son, Aurangzeb, and imprisoned for the rest of his life in the Red Fort at Agra, where he died a broken man. He was never allowed to look directly upon the white Taj again, by his son, but was allowed to see it in a reflection in a diamond in the wall of his prison," explained the guide.

"What a terrible thing to do to your father. What had he done to make his son hate him so much?" asked Mel, with tears in her eyes.

"No one ever knew Madam," said the guide.

They went from the Taj to the Red Fort where the guide showed them the single room prison. He explained how the ex-ruler had been chained to the wall so that he could not look directly on his beloved Taj Mahal.

"Why is there a wall, then a deep wide grassy part, and then the main wall of the fort?" asked Masood.

"This Sir was where the tigers and snakes lived," explained the guide.

"What for?" continued Masood.

"In many forts, they have water in this part. Water was not plentiful here so they put wild animals in there so that if anyone tried to invade the fort, the animals would get them, or it would slow the invaders down. The defenders could then pour hot oil on them and fire arrows or stones and rocks".

"Ugh!! Your people certainly knew how to be horrible to others didn't they?" shuddered Mel.

"Yes Madam. It was kill or be killed and they had it down to a great skill. Are you staying in Agra?" asked the guide.

"No," replied Masood.

"Then it is getting late, and I would suggest you leave as soon as possible."

They took the guide's advice, paid him with a handsome tip, and found the taxi waiting nervously for them at the entrance to the Red Fort.

"We should be going," the taxi driver urged Masood as they approached. "It will be dark soon and it is better we travel while it is light."

On the journey back, they began to notice abandoned cars at intervals along the road, and the driver was driving faster than he had on the way to Agra in the morning. After a near miss with a cow crossing the road, Masood asked the driver to slow down.

"Sorry Sir, but I must go as fast as I can, and not slow for anything," replied the driver, who was panicking.

It was nearly dark now and the speed of the car seemed manic.

"Slow down damn you. We want to get to Delhi alive," shouted Masood.

"Then you will please to let me concentrate and do my job," replied the driver. Masood, who was in the front, pulled on the handbrake hard and the car skidded and shuddered to a reluctant halt.

"What is wrong with you man? You are driving like the devil is after you," shouted Masood.

"For all I know he may be," said the driver in a shaky voice.

"What do you mean?" demanded Masood.

"Bandits," said the driver.

"Bandits!!! What fucking bandits? Where?" shouted Cindy.

"There are bandits on this road and they wait for any car foolish enough to travel at night, and that is what happened to all the cars you saw earlier," stuttered the driver. His eyes wide with growing fear.

"Idiot! You should have told us this before. We must go back to Agra," insisted Masood.

"No Sir," said the now petrified driver. "There is a village, a few miles on, and we will be safe there."

"How do you know that?" demanded Masood.

"Because the army is there and they will be collecting convoys to escort. We can join one of those," answered the driver.

The crack of the rifle shot was enough to settle the discussion, and the taxi hurtled off down the road to the distant village. At the entrance to the village, was an army officer. He motioned them to stop.

"Where are you going?"

"Delhi Sir," said the shaken driver.

"Not tonight you're not. There has been an ambush ten miles on and we cannot clear the road until morning," advised the officer.

"Is there a hotel here?" asked Masood.

"Yes Sir," replied the officer. "But it is full. You are best to park up by those trucks over there and sleep in your car. We will tell you when it is safe to travel."

It was a restless night for them all, and the soldiers constantly checking the vehicles around them did not help. But it was soon morning. They found the village café open and doing a good trade with the truck drivers, and other stranded travellers.

It was around eleven in the morning when they were told they could use the road again. When they passed the site of the ambush, it was clear the truck driver and the travellers in the car behind had stood little chance. The truck cab was riddled with bullet holes, and so was the car. The truck body was empty.

The bandits had not had it all their own way either. Three of them were hanging from trees by the side of the road. They had clearly been surprised by the army and been killed in a gun fight, but had been hung up with messages scrawled on them to warn others.

It was late in the afternoon when they arrived back at the hotel to be greeted by a relieved manager.

"Welcome back. We thought the bandits had got you. There was news that they had killed a car full of people on the Agra road last night," said the manager.

Masood suspected he was more worried about who would pay the outstanding bill than for their safety, but the girls thought the welcome back warm and sincere.

"Thank God that's over, Masood. If I ever say I have always wanted to visit somewhere again, just ignore me," said an exhausted Cindy.

"That goes for me too," said Mel.

"Was it not worth it to see the Taj Mahal?" joked Masood.

"If I had been told before we went what may happen, then you could have kept the Taj," retorted Cindy, heading for the shower. "I'm going to try and get clean. If it's ever going to be possible to be clean again."

"I'll join you my love," replied Masood.

"Not this time lover. I may be a long time," Cindy replied.

Mel and Ali had already gone when Masood looked around the suite to find he was alone. He fixed himself a large scotch and settled on a deep settee. The sound of the glass breaking on the floor woke him up with a start. He must have dozed off and it had fallen from his relaxing grip. Cindy eventually came out of the shower. He had a hot shower before dinner.

It was a reflective group who ate dinner together that night, but none more than Masood, who could not shake off the thought of what a disaster would have befallen the Middle East, if they had been the travellers who had been killed.

After dinner, they all agreed a good night's sleep was what they needed, and retired for an early night.

"Ali, did you know that road was so dangerous?" asked Mel.

"No, my love. I would never knowingly place you in danger like that, I promise. Now let's get some sleep. We are going somewhere nice tomorrow," promised Ali.

"Where?" asked Mel.

"You will see my love. It will be worth the wait," Ali replied.

CHAPTER NINE
Old Fashioned Luxury

They all had breakfast and then left for the airport.

"Where are we going Masood? You must tell us, it's not fair," demanded Cindy.

Masood was enjoying keeping the girls in suspense when Cindy's handbag hit him on the back of the head.

"Tell us now or I get out at the next junction and walk back to the hotel," demanded Cindy.

Masood laughed. "The beggars will get you Cindy."

"I don't care. You know I'll do it you bastard," challenged Cindy.

"Ok. We're going to Kashmir," Masood gave in.

"Wow," said Mel. "I've always wanted to go to...." Before she finished, she realized they were all staring at her. "Sorry!" she bleated to roars of laughter from the other three.

After the complaints about the flight from Bombay, Masood had hired a private jet, and they were soon above the clouds.

"Will it always be like this Ali?" Mel asked.

"If that is what you want my love, yes," replied Ali, reaching for her hand in reassurance.

They ate a light lunch on the flight and it seemed no time at all before they were landing. Masood gave instructions to the pilot to be back in two days and they were soon in a taxi bound for their houseboat.

"A houseboat, how romantic" cooed Cindy, "What will you think of next Masood. Are you going soft in your old age, or are you taking lessons from Ali?"

"Neither. I just thought it would be a nice way to spend a few days before we leave India," answered Masood, smiling.

They arrived at the lake and were soon on a water-ferry to their house-boat. The girls were chattering like monkeys.

"This one is yours Sir," announced the ferryman pulling alongside the front of a large flat-topped wooden barge painted in bright colours.

The houseboy appeared from inside to help them aboard and take their luggage. He gave them a guided tour of the boat and left them to choose their bedrooms, whilst he started lunch.

The boat was huge with four large bedrooms, a saloon and a small bathroom for each bedroom. Each bedroom contained an enormous bed, a dressing table and two chairs. The boat's roof also doubled as a sundeck. They bathed and changed for lunch, which was served in the saloon with long cool drinks to start.

"Have you tried the bed yet?" asked an excited Mel.

"None of your bloody business," joked a smiling Cindy.

"No, you know what I mean. They're so deep you just sink into them. It's wonderful," continued Mel slightly embarrassed.

"I know," winked Cindy. "Bloody fantastic. I don't know how we'll manage naughties, but who cares," she laughed.

"Well I do, for one," laughed Masood.

After lunch they chatted like old school friends for the rest of the after-noon, and listened to the crickets on the bank which the boat was moored to. It was nice to relax after the recent dangers and they all appreciated a little chill-out time.

"With your permission Sir," it was the soft voice of the houseboy Ahmed who interrupted Masood's thoughts, "I will be cooking a lamb Pasanda for dinner, unless you have another wish?"

Masood glanced around and they all nodded agreement.

"Sounds delicious Ahmed," smiled Masood.

They were all dozing in the comfortable old chairs when the smell of dinner began to waft through to the saloon.

"God that smells fantastic," chirped up Mel.

"Hope it's nearly ready. I'm starving," said Masood.

"You're always bloody starving," teased Cindy. "Let's have a drink be-fore dinner she urged."

Without hesitation Ali was up and at the bar, taking orders like a waiter.

With perfect timing, Ahmed announced dinner just as they had finished their drinks.

"Wow," said Mel. "This is wonderful."

"Thank you madam," answered Ahmed. "For dessert there is a choice of trifle or ice cream."

Everyone chose trifle. They chatted over coffee and went to bed about ten o'clock. Within minutes, they were all in a deep, restful sleep.

Morning came and with it, the smell of breakfast cooking.

"God I'm hungry," announced Ali as he came out of the bedroom in just his underpants, through the saloon to the front of the boat and dived straight into the lake. He surfaced with a big grin on his face. "Anyone for a swim?" he shouted.

"Not likely," said Cindy. "I like to eat before I drown."

Ali laughed and set off to swim to the far shore.

"Come back Ali," shouted Mel. "You don't know what is in the water."

"Oh, it's safe my love," shouted Ali turning to face her. Then with a cry for help he vanished underwater.

"Oh God not again," cried Mel, diving off the front of the boat and swimming as fast as she could to the spot where he had disappeared. She arrived just as he surfaced smiling.

"Hello my love. Fancied a swim after all?" he grinned.

"You swine, I'm going to kill you, Ali Beg," screeched Mel.

"You have to catch me first," he said, swimming out of reach. She swam a few strokes then lunged at him grabbing his manhood.

"Now you are mine, Beg. Come with me," said Mel as she swam with one hand back to the boat, not letting him go.

"You're going to pull it off Mel," Ali begged.

"Oh, so you can read minds as well now can you?" asked Mel.

"No my love, no, I was only having a joke," pleaded Ali.

"Yes, I know. But I dived in to save you and now I am wet in white undies which means when I get out the world will see my bits," said Mel.

"I did not think my love. I'm sorry, and they are such lovely bits," Ali pleaded.

"Yes Ali, your brains are in your dick and that's why I'm not letting go," promised Mel.

Masood and Cindy were by now laughing and fit to burst. "Coming aboard Mel?" asked Masood stretching out his hand and not taking his eyes from her.

"Not while you're staring at me you dirty old man. Get me a robe please," shouted Mel.

"What and miss the show?" he grinned.

Smack!!! Cindy's hand hit the back of his head.

"Get the bloody robe you dirty old sod," ordered Cindy. He trotted off to get a robe and was back moments later.

"Now, go inside and have a cold shower while I help Mel out," ordered Cindy. He grinned and went meekly inside. He didn't care about seeing Mel. It was all just good fun.

After breakfast, they spent the morning on the roof of the boat, soaking up the sun and sipping long cool drinks whilst a procession of hawkers tried to sell them a vast array of local craft goods from beautiful rugs to lovingly carved wooden statues, trays and ornate brassware.

In the afternoon, they caught the water-taxi and went ashore, then caught a taxi up into the mountains to look at the fantastic scenery.

"Ali, I am in heaven," said Mel.

"We are high Mel, but not that high," joked Ali.

They drank tea at the roadside café and then took a path to a waterfall and watched the crystal clear water sparkle on its long fall into the small lake below, where it turned blue and silver and shimmered in the bright afternoon sun.

"What is that building over there?" Ali asked the taxi driver/guide.

"That is the border post with Pakistan, and sometimes you can hear the guards shooting at each other," answered the taxi driver.

"Why?" asked Mel.

"Oh, there are often border fall-outs. Each country jealously guards its section of Kashmir. It lasts for a few days then it's over for a while," explained the driver.

They returned down the stony path strewn with small rocks which had fallen from the hills above.

"It is sad Ali, that even in a place as peaceful and beautiful as this, men are still trying to kill each other for a bit of rock," reflected Mel.

"Yes my love it is," agreed Ali.

They returned to the houseboat for dinner and talked into the small hours before retiring. The dawn broke and was announced by the birds singing. It was a beautiful day and when Ali and Mel finally emerged, it was to the sight of Masood and Cindy swimming and playing in the lake. Without hesitation, they joined them and a water fight ensued between the two couples, with much splashing and laughing. They climbed back onto the boat when breakfast was announced by Ahmed, the houseboy. After breakfast, Mel and Ali returned to bed for a nap they claimed, but the noises from the bedroom were nothing like snoring.

That afternoon, they flew back to Delhi in the chartered jet and returned to their hotel to find a letter waiting for Masood. As always, he opened it in private then made a phone call. After this, he came back to the lounge and announced that they would be leaving in the morning for Amsterdam.

It was no surprise that the girls were getting used to this routine, and knew better than to protest or moan. They spent the evening seeing the sights of Delhi, and throwing the hundreds of coins Masood had obtained, through the open taxi window to the beggars at the road junctions.

CHAPTER TEN
Death in the Land of Tulips

They caught the mid morning KLM flight and were in Amsterdam that evening.

"I could get used to this first class travel," joked Cindy.

"Yes," agreed Mel. "If I have to, I will."

The hotel in Amsterdam was not as sumptuous as the hotel in Delhi, or the Hilton in Dubai, but it was still excellent, and their suite was luxurious.

"Shall we eat in or out?" inquired Masood. They all agreed to eat in, as they were tired.

They had the food cooked in their suite and it was delicious. After dinner, they drank a little and the wine soon took its toll. It was not long before they headed for bed and were all sound asleep.

"Come on you lot. Out of bed!" shouted Masood, knocking on the door of Ali and Mel's bedroom.

"What's the panic?" asked Mel stumbling through the door. "I booked a tour guide and car for ten o'clock and we're late," replied Masood.

"We haven't even had breakfast yet," replied Mel. They were all rushing around like mad things when the phone rang.

"I have a tour guide waiting for you Sir," the receptionist told Ali.

"Please ask them to wait, and we will be down in a few minutes," said Ali, trying to put on his shirt and hold the phone to his ear at the same time. They arrived in reception a little breathless, to be met by a very smartly dressed guide.

"Good morning. I am your guide, Heidi."

"We're sorry we're late," apologized Mel for them all.

"No trouble at all," was Heidi's reply. "Please follow me out to the bus." They did, where the driver was holding the door open for them to get in.

The bus windows were tinted for privacy of the occupants. Although it was large enough to have fifteen seats, there were only six seats in the passenger area, but what seats! Deep, comfortable cushions, and high backs with armrests for maximum comfort, and they all swivelled a full 360 degrees.

"Mmm," said Masood, as he entered the bus, "very nice indeed."

"Thank you Sir," smiled Heidi as he passed her. "This is our driver, Hans. We will be touring the main sites and if there is anywhere you wish to stop, please tell me as we are at your disposal for the day," Heidi confirmed.

They set off with Heidi giving a running commentary on places they were passing, and recommending a place for lunch. This was the best part of the tour yet. They were all starving and the food was very good. They continued the tour and towards late afternoon were in the red light district.

"What are you laughing at Ali?" asked Mel.

"Women are sitting in the windows of the houses or standing in the doorways half naked. Is it legal? I thought Europeans were very straight laced about these things," answered a bemused Ali.

"Oh yes Sir," said Heidi. "We are very open minded in Holland and the women have to have regular medical checks. It is all properly controlled so there is no danger for the clients, and no danger for the women."

Ali just shook his head in amazement.

"Why? Do you fancy one of them Ali?" challenged Mel. "Are you getting tired of me already," she joked not smiling.

"No my love," said Ali. "Honest you are more than enough woman for me."

"Do you think this would work in London?" Masood asked.

"I doubt it," replied Cindy. "The pimps wouldn't like it at all. It would affect their earnings and control of the girls too much."

At the end of the tour, they were taken back to the hotel. Masood gave Heidi and Hans a good tip. They went up to the suite to bathe and change for an evening out. Ali was still breaking out in fits of the giggles about the women in the red light district.

"Want to go and try one?" asked Mel hardly hiding her annoyance.

"No my love," Ali protested, "I have all the woman I can handle right here. It just seems funny to see them in their underwear, on display in the windows and standing at the doors of their houses."

"Good," was her only reply as she headed for the shower. Ali offered to scrub her back and she pulled him in the shower still fully clothed. They lost track of the time and when they came out, Masood and Cindy had been ready some time. They had left and gone down to the bar.

"Sorry," they announced as they entered the bar.

"Ali felt he had to apologize, and I let him make it up to me for this afternoon," explained Mel.

"Wish I had thought of that," said Masood. "I got the name of a great Thai restaurant from Heidi and have booked us in. There is also a good nightclub we can go to later." They all agreed this was a good idea and after another drink, left for the restaurant.

"Hope the food is good, I'm starving. Never had Thai food before," said Cindy.

"Good evening ladies and gentlemen. We have you down for a private room upstairs," said the head waiter as he met them at the door. "Please follow me." They were shown to a large room with a good view of the canal, with its busy water traffic, and many couples walking the cobbled streets on either side.

"This is lovely Masood," said Mel.

"Let's hope the food is as good," came in Ali. "What shall we have to drink?" he asked.

"May I try Kir Royale?" asked Mel.

"Sound's good. But what is it?" asked Ali.

The waiter jumped in "Champagne and cassis Sir, that's a strong black-currant liqueur."

"Then let's all try it," suggested Masood. They all also ordered a starter but could not agree on a main course.

"It all sounds so good. Why don't we all pick two dishes each?" suggested Ali.

"That's a great idea, we can have a feast," replied Mel excitedly.

"Are you sure you want all this food Sir?" asked the waitress, clearly concerned that they would waste a lot and may not want to pay the bill later.

"Yes that's right," said Masood. The waitress returned with the head waiter.

"I just wish to confirm my waitress has not made a mistake Sir," said the head waiter, with concern in his voice. "It is not a problem, but we will have to lay another table as well. It is a lot of food." Masood confirmed the order and with a snap of the head waiter's fingers, staff appeared by magic with a second table and covers. They were busy chatting and eating their starter when the main course started to arrive, and it kept on coming and coming.

"We will never eat all this," protested Mel.

"No, but we can give it a damn good try," laughed Masood. Two hours later, they gave up. It had been a valiant effort, but the food had beaten them in the end.

They sat for another hour, talking and commenting on the people passing by underneath their window. The music of an accordion wafted in from across the street, adding to the atmosphere of enjoyment.

"Shall we go to the club now?" suggested Ali. "I could do with dancing that lot off."

In minutes, they had paid the bill, left a good tip, and were in a taxi on the way to La Trocadero. When the taxi drew up outside, there was a queue at the entrance. Masood beckoned one of the doormen. Over came a huge man with a bald head, except for a short pony tail at the back. He bent over and looked in through the open window of the taxi at Masood.

"Do we have to wait?" Masood asked glancing from the doorman's face to the wad of notes in his hand and back again to the doorman's face.

"No Sir," said the doorman, smiling and opening the door, while taking the wad from Masood's hand with practiced ease. He spoke into his headset and they were shown straight past the waiting queue.

"What would you like to drink?" asked the waiter, who showed them to a table at the edge of the dance floor.

"Kir Royale for all," ordered Masood without conferring.

"Nice shout," said Cindy.

"Shout. What is nice shout?" asked Ali.

"It means well done, or spot on," retorted Cindy, and they all burst out laughing.

After several drinks, Ali was brave enough to dance. He also wanted to snuggle into Mel's breasts. He had been watching them heave all night and he wanted to feel them heave against his head. Cindy soon had Masood dancing and the dance floor was filling up. Masood was so busy feeling pleased with himself for arranging such a nice evening he didn't even see the punch coming. Whack!!!

"That's what all you rich bastards deserve," crowed his assailant standing over the very still body of Masood. "We queue for hours and you just get straight in with your money and power."

Cindy exploded, kicking the assailant straight in the groin. Caught totally by surprise, he went down hard but she was not finished. She kicked him in the mouth and the breaking of teeth was a noise to remember. He was screaming now, with his groin on fire. Blood and broken teeth spewing from the ragged hole in his face where his mouth had been, and she was about to stamp her stiletto through his temple when Mel grabbed her.

"No! Babe no," shouted Mel. "He's not worth it," she pleaded holding tight to a struggling Cindy.

The bouncers arrived, scooped up the injured man and were gone. The floor had cleared and Masood was coming around. The staff cleared up the mess and the band struck up to get the dancing started again.

The bouncers threw the man out into the street and minutes later, still screaming, he was taken away in a police van.

"Whachhh happened?" asked a drunken Ali.

"It's ok Ali," assured Mel finally easing her grip on Cindy.

"Bollocks it's alright," came in Masood. "I was enjoying that dance," he laughed. A free set of drinks arrived to ease the pain in Masood's jaw and cool Cindy down. They left soon after and returned to the hotel, where Cindy was gentle with Masood that night.

"What the hell were you doing Swami?" demanded Saeed. "You are there to ensure he does not get hurt. Our masters will not forgive us, any of us, if he gets hurt or killed."

"It happened so quickly. The man he came from nowhere. I had no time to do anything," explained Swami.

"You're a useless bastard," shouted Khalaf, rising from his seat.

"Fuck off you big bastard," retorted Swami, pulling out a knife. Its blade glinted in the light from the chandelier above their heads as he moved.

He never got to use it. Moving at tremendous speed for a huge man, Khalaf was across the room and had grabbed Swami. He picked him up like a doll and while turning, threw Swami the full width of the room. The cracking noise as Swami's body collided with the wall said it all. He hit the floor in a heap and lay still, his head at an impossible angle. Death had been instantaneous.

"Good riddance," said Riad. "You were right, he was useless."

Saeed was more bothered, that they were now a man short, than that Swami was dead. None of them checked for signs of life, they had all seen enough death to know he was dead. Saeed made a phone call, and by morning Swami's body was on the way back home and his replacement was on the way. On arrival, the new man was whisked to the hotel and introduced to everyone not on duty.

"Pleased to meet you all, said the new man. I am Mayoub and I am honoured to work with you all on this most important of missions."

"Just hope you're more useful than that other creature," growled Khalaf.

"Yes, my brother was not much use as anything, but a thief. He thought he was good with a knife, but I am better!" It was said in a way and a tone that left little doubt it was a warning.

It was a bright new day in Amsterdam and the sun streamed into the lounge as Masood, Ali, and Mel sat drinking their first coffee of the day.

"Is your head alright today Masood?" asked Mel.

"Yes, thank you. My jaw is a little sore, but not too bad," answered Masood, rubbing his jaw at the same time.

"Are you having breakfast?" asked Ali.

"Yes," replied Masood.

"Then it can't be hurting too much can it?" said Ali.

They had breakfast and went out for the day to visit a couple of the sights they had seen briefly the day before.

"Ali, I am sure those two men are following us," said Mel.

"Yes my love, I have explained. They are there to protect us," said Ali.

"So where were they last night?" snapped Cindy.

"Who needs them around when you're with me?" joined in Masood.

"Who said I will always be around, lover?" replied Cindy.

"Don't even joke about that," said Masood. "I thought you loved me."

"No. You asked me if I loved you," replied Cindy, "and I haven't made my mind up yet."

"Oh, so it's not a no then. Well, not yet anyway," Masood winked.

"You two are winding us up aren't you?" asked Ali.

"The penny has dropped, as they say," confirmed Masood.

"I don't know if I love the sod," protested Cindy. "But he floats my boat and that's all that matters."

Mel hugged Cindy so hard they were all waiting for the snap.

"Hey, I can't breathe." Cindy gasped.

By now, they had forgotten about Asif and Yousef. They were not aware of the other men watching them from some distance behind, as he and his partner had been with them for many days now and preferred to stay in the shadows.

CHAPTER ELEVEN
Who Minds the Minders

Kaleel and Majeed were from Libya and had instructions not to make contact with anyone, but to watch what everyone did, and report back. Kaleel had a face you would not forget in a hurry. He had lost one eye in a knife fight, and the same slash had left him with a jagged scar from scalp to chin. It had the effect of making his cruel grin look very sinister. Majeed's sole memorable feature was a huge nose, even by Arab standards, it was huge.

They did not realize it, but Asif had spotted them the day before, and had reported back to Saeed who had decided that they should be left alone for the moment unless they posed a threat. If, or when that happened, they should be dealt with. He too had reported back, but had been told not to do anything. Negotiations were taking place with a view to persuading Libya to remove them, or join forces, and an inter-Arab incident was not in anyone's interests.

That evening, Masood, Ali and the girls ate in the suite preferring not to go out after the previous night's excitement. They were tired and all wanted an early night.

"Now I have you alone Cindy Harker, are you going to stay with me or is this just a game to you?" Masood winked.

"So it's a game you're after. I thought you would have had enough fun and games last night," replied Cindy.

"I don't remember any fun. My jaw aches too much for there to have been too many games," said Masood as he laughed. "Just don't do to me what you did to that poor bastard last night." He grinned glancing around the room in feigned innocence.

"How do you know what I did to that poor bastard? You swine. You were faking it all along. You weren't knocked out," complained Cindy.

Masood was writhing with laughter.

"You saw it all."

"Yes my love and you were very good. Poor sod never knew what hit him," his ribs starting to hurt from laughing.

"And neither will you," she whooped, diving on him and beating him with her fists. She was rough to him that night and he loved every minute. He had raised the passion in her and he would pay the price before morning.

"Do you have a lot of money Ali?" asked Mel.

"Depends what you call a lot," replied Ali.

"Well, where I come from a lot is enough to buy the club Masood bought," Mel replied.

"Oh that was pocket change," returned Ali.

"Big head," she joked.

"Does it make a difference?" asked Ali.

"I just wonder why we have men following us around everywhere. Are you afraid of being kidnapped, and if so, are Cindy and I in any danger?" asked Mel with concern in her voice.

"No," exclaimed Ali. "I promise you we will never be kidnapped. These men are here to guard us not harm us. I promise I will explain it all one day, but for now, please trust me. I will not let anyone harm a hair of your lovely head."

"That's fine. If you say so, but you must be very rich," said Mel.

Ali pulled her to him and stroked her long dark hair soothingly.

"Yes, I suppose we have about a billion dollars between us," he answered.

She was about to shout something, but he placed his fingers on her lips and whispered.

"Shsh. Money is nice, but we have each other and that is worth more." They made passionate love that night, but her words had brought questions to his mind that denied him peaceful sleep. He decided he had to talk things over with Masood in the morning.

In order for him to have time alone with Masood, Ali arranged a full body pamper for the girls in the hotel's beauty centre, which he announced at breakfast.

"That is so thoughtful of you Ali," said Mel. After breakfast, they left for the centre, leaving Masood and Ali alone.

"I have to talk something over with you. It has been worrying me for a few days now," said a worried Ali.

"About the girls' safety?" asked Masood.

"How did you know?" asked Ali.

"Ali, I can read you like a book. They are as safe as we are," replied Masood.

"But what if they decide to torture the girls instead of us?" asked Ali, with concern in his voice.

"That will do them no good. They know nothing," comforted Masood.

"No, I know that, but would you not tell them the secrets to save Cindy?" questioned Ali.

"Yes my friend, if I knew something, but I don't," answered Masood.

"You don't! Then who the hell does?" demanded Ali, his voice rising to a screech.

"I don't know! I don't know, we must trust Kutty," Masood replied. He placed a calming hand on his friend's shoulder.

"How can I trust a dead man?" challenged Ali.

"We must my friend, we must," answered Masood again squeezing Ali's shoulder.

On listening duty, Riad was getting very frustrated at the noises coming from the speaker.

"It is useless Saeed. I can't hear anything except hissing," said Riad.

"Yes, yes, they are not stupid. They have guessed we have them bugged and have gone into the shower to talk," confirmed Saeed.

"If we only had more time and knew which hotels they were going to, then I could do a better job of bugging the place," said Riad.

"Yes, but we don't so there's no use moaning. They will slip up soon enough. Don't worry and when they do we will be there to catch them, and have some fun," said Saeed, smiling.

Saeed was not happy about the situation and knew his men were getting sick of following duties. They were used to action, and nerves were getting frayed as had been shown when Khalaf killed Swami. He was pacing the room smiling, but it belied how he really felt.

"I could kidnap the women," offered Asif.

"What for? They know nothing and if they are hurt or killed, how do we know how Masood would react. He only has to miss out one lot of transmission information and we are all dead men," snapped Saeed, glaring at Asif, for his stupidity.

"How do we know he knows anything, how do we know there are any other bombs?" sneered Riad.

"We don't, and we have to wait for them to make a mistake. We know where the money is going to, and our citizens' safety is what matters for now, so we must play the long game and wait. Let them have their fun. It will be our turn soon enough," said Saeed. He was feeling just as frustrated as the rest were.

The girls returned late afternoon pampered and preened and looking more gorgeous than ever.

"Wow! Now that's what I call a great day's work. You look gorgeous Cindy," remarked Masood.

"Cheeky sod Masood. I was gorgeous before we went out. You'll pay for that later," Cindy said pulling a face at Masood.

"Promises, promises," was Masood's reply.

No one knew it yet, but it was to be their last night in Amsterdam.

Cindy made Masood pay for his cheek when they were alone later.

They were getting ready for breakfast when the phone rang. Masood answered it.

"Good morning Sir," said the cheerful receptionist. "I have a letter for you. Shall I send it up?"

"No, I will come down and collect it," said Masood. Cindy had heard and was getting to know the drill.

"Shall I pack?" she asked.

"Not yet. Probably later. Let's have breakfast when I get back. Will you order from room service for me and I will be back shortly?" asked Masood, kissing her forehead and heading for the door.

CHAPTER TWELVE
The Big Gamble

"Where to this time Masood?" asked Ali at breakfast.

"Is nothing I do private?" protested Masood, laughing. "Monte Carlo. We leave this afternoon." Their trip was to be a short one, as Masood had hired a private jet to ensure they arrived in style. He wanted to ensure Monte Carlo knew they were there.

His plan caused utter confusion with his followers. One minute they were in sight at the airport, the next they had gone.

"We shall get on the next flight anyway. They are bound to be on it, but under different names," stated Saeed confidently. They were not on it. It was a fiasco. After walking up and down both aisles, he announced that Masood's party was not on the plane, and asked if he and his men could get off. The cabin staff would not let them, and he could hardly explain what was wrong.

"Khalaf. You, Riad and Omar go and get the next flight. We will go on this one," ordered Saeed.

"Sir, I said no one was getting off this flight," said the Chief Steward.

"You have held us up long enough and the other passengers are getting worried," explained the Captain, arriving from the cockpit as Saeed was about to start an argument.

"Then let me call my Embassy," pleaded Saeed.

"It will make no difference, Sir. I say what happens on this aircraft and I am waiting to take off. Now please, sit down or you will be restrained for the duration," said the Captain. Saeed was visibly about to blow a gasket, but did as he was bid. The last thing he wanted was Aziz finding out he had caused an international incident, and lost his prey. If that happened, he was guaranteed to spend the rest of his life on a border post with Iraq.

"Where are we going Masood?" asked a confused Ali. "The check-in desk is over there."

"Yes, but we are not on that flight. We're going by private jet. Just follow this lady and don't ask any more questions," said Masood.

Ali did as he was told. The lady was one of their flight crew and she had a bottom that was made for a man to follow. It was contained just tightly enough in her uniform skirt and she walked with practiced perfection. She knew he was looking and she loved that feeling of power it gave her. She smiled to herself as she led the way to the aircraft.

Ali was enjoying the view when Mel grabbed him by the hair, lifting him from the floor.

"Is she better than me Ali?" she demanded glaring at him.

"No my love," he weakly replied.

"Good, if I catch you ogling her arse again, I'll stick you up it," promised a furious Mel.

Yes my love I, I…" said an embarrassed Ali.

"Don't apologize. You'll only make it worse," she growled. Ali liked this, as he had always liked strong-willed women and he had only just realized Mel was very strong-willed.

Masood had been looking at the stewardess too. All he got was a dig in the ribs from Cindy, and a look-but-don't-touch smile to go with the dig.

"We seem to have lost our bodyguards, Masood," said Mel, as the plane took off.

"Yes. I have given them the day off," Masood smirked. He could only imagine the trouble back at the airport, when the watchers realized they were missing, and he kept laughing for the entire flight.

"What do you keep laughing at Masood?" asked Ali.

"Oh, just you at the airport," replied Masood. "It was funny to see Mel pick you up like that."

"It wasn't funny," protested Ali. "I thought she was going to pull my hair out by the roots."

"If you look at her arse again, I will," threatened Mel. "And it won't be the hair on your head either."

"What a woman," was all Masood could say.

They were all impressed by the flight and the service, but when the stewardess brought the drinks, she got a glare from Mel that would have stripped paint. Upon landing, they were met by a limousine and driven straight to the hotel.

"This is the way to travel," commented Ali.

"Yes, I agree," chirped in Masood. "Perhaps we should buy a jet of our own," he laughed.

"Are you trying to impress us, or are you just showing off?" Cindy asked.

"No. We have a lot of travelling to do for a long time, and it would make more sense to have our own transport, ready when we are, as it were," said Masood.

"Show off," was Cindy's reply.

"Will we really have our own plane, Masood?" asked Ali.

"We can talk about it later. For now I need a nap," answered Masood, closing his eyes. Ali knew there was to be no nap for Masood. He had to make it up to Cindy for his indiscretion at the airport, and Ali thought it was time he took Mel shopping for something special.

"Honestly Ali, you don't have to buy me a ring or ask me to marry you. I went a bit mad this afternoon when I saw you watching that tart and I'm sorry," said Mel.

"I don't want to buy it because of that," said Ali. "I want to show the whole world we are in love, or would you be ashamed to wear my ring?"

"Don't be daft," Mel defended. "Of course, I would be proud to wear your ring, and to marry you if you really want me to."

They were, by now, naked on the big round bed.

Ali blinked just once. "Yahoo," he yelled, startling her and heading for the door.

"Ali!!!" shouted Mel, but he was out of the suite and running along corridors and down staircases. He was so busy shouting the good news to everyone he met, he forgot he was naked. Most men looked on in envy. He was semi-erect during his run, and it looked as if he had two and a half legs. Many of the women looked on in envy too, and at least two of the blue-rinse brigade required smelling salts after he passed by. He made it to the street before the doorman tripped him and threw his overcoat over him.

The journey back upstairs took longer than the one coming down, as he stopped to apologize to the bewildered residents and visitors of the hotel. He was wearing a face as red as a ripe tomato. It must have been fate that some of the paparazzi were waiting around outside the hotel when he emerged. It certainly made it easier for Saeed to find Masood and party when they got to Monte Carlo. The smile on Mel's face was all he wanted to see when he got back to the suite.

"I am so sorry," apologized Ali.

"What for?" giggled Mel.

"No one has ever flashed the jet set of Monte Carlo for me before. You have nothing to be ashamed of, quite the opposite. I bet you and your middle leg will be the talk of the casino tonight my love," laughed Mel.

"Yes but…," started Ali.

"No buts. We have had enough excitement for today. Let's relax and get some drinks sent up. We can go out tonight and try the casino, as long as you wear a false beard," Mel teased.

Masood and Cindy had missed all the fun and took great pleasure, later that day, listening to Mel's story, and pulling Ali's leg.

"Look Ali, you're famous. You're on the evening news," teased Cindy.

"Oh my God," laughed Mel.

"You will have to fight the women off with a big stick Mel," said Masood, laughing loudly with tears streaming down his cheeks.

"Did you say STICK?" teased Cindy, bursting into uncontrollable laughter. By now, Ali was as red as a beetroot and the other three couldn't stop laughing.

"I can't go out now," Ali protested.

"Of course you can. You will be a celebrity everywhere. No wonder you have been looking like the cat that got the cream for the last few weeks Mel," continued Cindy. "Lucky bitch!"

They ate in the hotel restaurant that night where Ali glowed like a red light bulb for the entire meal. During the meal, Masood received a note, which he read and, excusing himself, stormed out of the room. He was not gone long and returned looking a lot calmer.

"Anything wrong, Masood?" asked Ali.

"Nothing my friend, nothing," assured Masood. He was inwardly seething. He had been summoned by the General Manager who had made it clear Ali's behaviour was not acceptable in his hotel and they must leave in the morning. He was determined it was not going to spoil their evening at the tables or their meal. After dinner, three of them retired to the bar whilst Masood went to the suite.

"I have to make a phone call, but I will not be long," said Masood. True to his word, he was back in about thirty minutes, and they left for the casino.

"How do you play roulette Ali?" asked Mel.

"Just place the chips on any number you like. Or you can do what he is doing and put them at the cross line of four numbers. There are lots of combinations, or you can just bet red or black," explained Ali.

"I will watch for a while and see what other people do," said Mel.

"Me too," agreed Cindy.

"Good idea," said Ali, turning and starting to head for the blackjack tables. She grabbed his arm.

"Where do you think you're going?" asked Mel.

"I was going to play blackjack my love. Why?" asked Ali, somewhat confused.

"Don't tell me you haven't noticed all the women in here eyeing you up," said Mel smiling.

"No" he protested, smiling weakly and noticing, for the first time, that there was a more than usual proportion of women around the roulette table. They were not watching the roulette wheel. He suddenly felt very vulnerable, like a sheep with a pack of wolves.

"Don't worry Ali," chirped in Cindy. "We girls will protect you." Ali laughed nervously.

He had no fear of any man, but he was on unknown ground here and it unsettled him.

"Didn't I see you on the evening news big boy?" asked a bubbly blonde standing next to him. At the same time, she was running her hand around the inside of his thigh.

"Yes you did," replied Mel. "And if you put your hand on him again, I'll break it off," she said, in a honey-sweet, but dripping-with-menace voice.

"Sorry my dear," replied the blonde. "Didn't realize he was spoken for. Can't blame a girl for trying can you?"

"Not at all," smiled Mel sweetly, carefully placing her foot on the blonde's left foot and trying to crush it into the thick carpet. Blondie winced, extricated her foot, and moved out of range.

Masood watched all this with great amusement. Ali had never had attention like this from women, and he was tickled to see how his friend coped with it all.

Mel and Cindy had decided to pool their money and bet together. They placed their first bet on twenty-eight, as they were both that age. With mounting excitement, they watched the wheel spin and the little ball hurtle around in the opposite direction. It came down off the polished wooden track, bounced several times, and settled on twenty-eight. The croupier smiled and pushed a stack of bright red chips next to their pile on twenty eight. Cindy reached over and grabbed them.

"What now?" asked Mel.

"Your birth date," suggested Cindy placing half the chips on twenty-nine. The girls were engrossed and excited now, and Ali took his chance to follow Masood to the blackjack tables.

He knew he had a following, but he had come here to gamble and was not prepared to risk losing Mel over any of the women in here tonight. They had mixed fortunes at blackjack, and Ali could not concentrate due to all the admiring glances he was getting from the throng of ladies around the table. This attention was also starting to get on other gamblers' nerves, and hostility towards Ali could be cut with a blunt knife. A tall, willowy, redhead standing at the other end of the table opposite Ali, was making it clear to everyone she was ready and willing to have Ali there and then on the table, by constantly looking him up and down, licking her pouting red lips and smiling provocatively. She was only small breasted, but if she got any more excited the dress was going to come apart at the seams.

"Ok doll, so he's built like a horse, but you're not getting to ride him," said a brash-voiced Texan grabbing her arm and hauling her away. "Doll, where I come from, you leave with the fella who brung ya," he drawled over her protests.

Masood had, meanwhile, got lucky and his seat was the hot one at the table.

"What is the table limit?" he inquired of the croupier.

"There is no limit Sir." Masood had the green light and started betting on three hands at a time in large amounts. He must have been ahead by around a hundred thousand dollars, when his luck changed and he lost it all and some more as well.

A buzz was rising in the casino as it does when someone is doing well. Every gambler wants to beat the house, but if it's not their night they are more than happy to cheer on whomever's luck is in.

At the roulette table, it was Cindy and Mel who were causing the buzz.

"How much do we have now?" asked Cindy.

"Never count your winnings while you're at the table," an elderly gentleman next to them piped up. "It's bad luck."

"Oh thank you," replied Mel. "Shall we put half on the next number?" asked Mel very excitedly. They nodded in agreement and pushed the brightly coloured chips on to number one. They wouldn't all fit, but the croupier gave them a helpful nod telling them he knew what the bet was.

Round again went the wheel and off went the ball. It felt like a long time before it came to rest and they dare not look. But a gasp from the assembled crowd announced they had won again. The croupier pushed over thirty-six very large grey chips, to their pile on number one.

"Is that all we won?" snapped Cindy.

"Oui Madame," smiled the croupier.

"Each of those is worth the same as the pile you bet," advised the old gentleman. You have about four hundred thousand pounds on the table at the moment," he advised.

"Oh God Cindy," said Mel reaching for the chips. "What shall we bet on next, and shall we bet it all?" she asked.

"I don't know doll," replied Cindy.

"No more bets," the croupier announced, as he started spinning the wheel and sending the little white ball on its journey around the outer track.

"But?" started Mel, looking pleadingly at the croupier.

"The bet is one I believe Madame," he advised firmly.

"The wheel was now spinning and the little ivory ball racing as well. A deathly hush fell on the assembled spectators. For Mel and Cindy, the room became surreal as each of them realized they could lose all their money because they were talking. Mel was shouting at the croupier, but he took no notice of her protests. It went on for hours, or at least it felt like it did, and time seemed to stand still. They dare not look, they were too upset. To have won so much, and now possibly lost it because they were too busy chatting would be devastating.

Ping went the ball. Ping, ping, ping.

The room was totally silent as it landed. "Congratulations Mesdames," said the soft voice of the croupier. The words were drowned out by the gasps and cheers of the crowd. Cindy opened her eyes to see the glorious little white ball nestling in number one. Gentle hands and arms were picking Mel up off the floor.

"Don't you touch that ball," shouted Cindy, glaring at the croupier. Around the table, uproar had broken out, with people talking about how much they had won, and reaching to shake their hands hoping some luck may rub off on contact. An enormous stack of chips arrived, as did the floor manager, pushing his way through the crowd.

"Do you wish to continue ladies he asked?"

"No," replied Mel weakly.

"Then if you would follow me ladies, we have champagne at the bar for you." They went with him leaving the buzz at the table behind.

"How much have we won?" asked Mel.

"You're English Madame?" he asked smiling at them.

"Yes," Mel confirmed.

"Around fifteen million pounds sterling," was his calm reply. It was some time before the smelling salts worked on them and they came around to find Ali and Masood smiling down at them.

"We hear you have had a good night girls," laughed Masood. "What does it feel like to be rich bitches?"

"It must be a dream. It can't be true," protested Cindy, looking at Mel for confirmation. Mel was ghostly white and was too busy crying to confirm anything.

"Is it true? Did we really win all that money, or are you going to tell us there is a limit on winnings?" asked Cindy.

"No Madame. We are proud to have no limit, and we have a reputation to protect. I have your cheque here for you, but would you be happy to allow photographs to be taken for the press tomorrow?" asked the floor manager.

"Yes, yes," they replied in unison. He handed them the cheque.

"We can, of course, split the cheque any way you wish. This is just for you to see what you have won," said the manager. They looked at the cheque in total disbelief. Fifteen million two hundred and fifty two thousand pounds. They read it again and again. This could not be true.

"You know Ali, I had a really strange dream last night," said Mel, on waking up.

"Did you my love?" teased Ali.

"Yes. It was one of those that seemed so real, and in it Cindy and I won a fortune at the casino," said Mel.

"Shame it wasn't real," teased Ali playing along with her dream theory.

"Still, it's nice to dream and sometimes they do come true you know. You haven't forgotten you have an appointment in an hour, have you my love?" he was laughing.

"With the press at the casino," Mel gasped. "So it was true!"

"It certainly was, and last time I looked you and Cindy were millionaires," smiled Ali lovingly.

"Ali what will we do with all that money?" asked Mel with excitement in her voice.

"I'm sure you will find something to buy, like a new pair of shoes. At least it will stop you having to sell yourself on the streets," joked Ali.

CHAPTER THIRTEEN
First Investment

They had breakfast together and were on the way out of the hotel when the duty manager stopped them.

"Sir," he said, addressing Masood. "I have instructions that you were leaving today and you have yet to settle your bill."

"That's because we're not leaving," was Masood's answer, as he headed for the door. The doorman barred the way.

"I spoke to you last night about this Sir," said the General Manager, from behind the reception counter. "I asked you and your party to leave because of the incident yesterday, and I must now insist that you pay your bill and leave. My staff will be happy to help you pack." Ali and the girls were now red with embarrassment, but Masood stood his ground.

"I thought your request a bit hasty last night and had hoped you would have reconsidered it by now," replied Masood calmly.

"I do not change my mind when I have made a decision Sir," replied the general manager. Other guests were now taking an interest in what was happening.

"And how long have you been the general manager here?" Masood asked.

"Fifteen years Sir. Why?"

"Yes, that's what I was told this morning," said Masood.

"By whom?" the indignant manager asked.

"By the previous owner, who by the way, thought highly of you," replied Masood.

"What do you mean the previous owner? This hotel has been in the same family for over seventy years," was the indignant question and reply from the confused general manager.

"Yes, but the operative word you are missing is previous. They no longer own it. I do and as my first action as new owner, you're dismissed!"

"No, no!! This is not possible," argued the general manager.

"It is the truth," confirmed Masood. "I tried to persuade you that my friend was drunk with joy, but you were so indignant that you would not listen. To add insult to injury, your summons spoiled my dinner. Now get out before I have you thrown out."

An insignificant man in a grey suit rose from his chair in the lobby and approached the now bewildered general manager, placing one arm around the manager's slumped shoulders.

"This cannot be true?" asked the manager, of the man in the suit.

"Yes it is my friend," replied the lawyer in the suit. "He signed the papers an hour ago and I have his draft in my pocket."

Devastated, the lawyer guided him to his suite where he packed. He had worked his way up from head waiter and now his career lay in ruins and all because of one mistake when he thought he was protecting the hotel's reputation.

"Do not worry my friend," comforted the lawyer. "You will have no trouble finding a new post." The assurance was not said with the greatest of conviction. Positions at this level were highly prized and jealously guarded.

"Masood, you did all that for me?" questioned a bewildered Ali.

"Yes Ali, I was not being treated like a naughty schoolboy by that idiot. So you gave a few old dears a thrill of a lifetime yesterday. Probably did them a world of good," said Masood.

"Yes, but it must have cost a fortune," replied Ali.

"It did my friend, but we should invest our money, and this place is a good investment," said Masood.

"Good God," butted in Cindy, "I thought we had lots of money, Mel.

"Come on you lot, we have the press to meet," urged an impatient Mel. There were more than just a few people at the presentation. There were a few celebrities and the general manager of the casino group.

"This is a fortune and yet you're smiling?" Mel asked him during a lull in the proceedings.

"Yes madam. It is good publicity for us. Big winners always encourage other people to gamble in the hope they will be as lucky. We will have recovered this by tomorrow, but the publicity is priceless my dear." She had never thought of it that way. After the ceremony, the huge cardboard cheques were taken back.

"As agreed, the money has already been transferred into your accounts in your English banks so there is no danger of anything getting lost ladies," said the general manager, still smiling.

"What are you going to do with your money Cindy?" asked Mel, on the way back to the hotel.

"First, I am going to find a public school for my son to go to, and pay the whole fees in advance," replied Cindy proudly.

"You have a son Cindy?" asked a shocked Masood.

"Yes. Johnny is seven," said Cindy.

"But you never mentioned him before," said Masood.

"There was no need to. I did not know how long we would last, and he is with his Gran, Sandra, at the moment, on holiday in Spain."

"What about you Mel. Have you any children?" asked a bemused Ali.

"No. Not been lucky enough to meet anyone I wanted to have children with," she replied. His face dropped. "Until now," she continued, smiling down at him and clutching him to her. His face was buried in her breasts, but if you could have seen it, he was beaming from ear to ear.

"I am going to buy a big boat," Mel announced. "There are some beautiful ones in the marina and I would like to go down there as soon as we can and see if there are any for sale."

That was enough for them all. Like a troupe of chattering monkeys, they diverted from the route to the hotel and took the limo down to the marina. It didn't take long to find the sales office or the smooth talking salesman who was only too delighted to congratulate them on their win.

"Do you have a boat or make in mind, Madame?" he asked.

"That one looks nice," was Mel's reply, looking at a picture of a fifty foot motor cruiser.

"The Sealine's a lovely handler. It's two years old with three double suites, saloon…", he rambled on and on. But it didn't matter; she had fallen in love with it anyway.

"Can we see it?" she interrupted him.

"Certainly Madam, please follow me." It was huge. The biggest boat Mel had ever been on was a rowing boat.

"Can we go out in it?" she asked.

"Of course Madam, but I need to arrange a crew for that, and I will have to get back to you with a time."

"That's fine we can do that tomorrow. Let's just look around it now," pleaded Mel, smiling.

It was a beautiful craft with polished wood and chrome everywhere, white leather seating in the saloon and all the comforts you could imagine including a well stocked bar. The suites were stunning. The first had a pale blue theme for the bedding and soft furnishings. The second was in shades of pink. The master suite was unbelievable with a giant circular bed filling the centre of the room surrounded by soft gold and purple silk furnishings. The carpet felt so thick it felt as if you were floating. The ceiling was made up of many mirrors reflecting the opulence of the room and making it seem even larger than it already was.

It took her breath away.

"I'll have it," Mel blurted out, taking everyone by surprise.

"But Madam, you have not tried it at sea," said the surprised salesman.

"Do you want to sell it or not?" Mel demanded.

"Yes Madam," he replied.

"Then I'll have it. Please arrange a crew for me. I want single men, who must be able and willing to go anywhere in the world when I want to. I assume it is capable of crossing oceans?" asked Mel.

"Oh yes Madam," confirmed the salesman.

"Then please have the paperwork at this hotel by tonight," ordered Mel.

"Are you sure about this?" asked a shocked Ali.

"Never so sure of anything in my life, lover," was Mel's reply, as she headed for the gangplank.

"It's a lot of money Mel. Two hundred thousand pounds," said Ali

"Worth it just to spend some time in that bed with you lover," was Mel's reply.

"You're beaming again Ali," said Masood.

"You'll have to stop making him smile Mel. He will be cracking mirrors all over our new hotel," laughed Masood.

The salesman couldn't believe his luck and had the papers at the hotel in record time. Mel had just made his week. In fact, with his commission on that sale, she made his month.

"They are making fools of us," protested Asif. "They are throwing money around like water and the world knows it's our money."

"It is not our money Asif. The decisions lie with our masters and they will tell us what to do. If you are not happy, you can always call home for instructions," sneered Riad.

"We have to wait our time Asif," counselled Omar.

"We will, as they say, have the last laugh in the end," said Omar."

CHAPTER FOURTEEN
The Second Installment

It was now a month since they left India and the first monthly payments were due. Masood had spent much of the afternoon on the phone to Geneva trying to find out which, if any, payments had been made.

"You look angry my friend," said Ali.

"I am. The bastards have not paid and the first month is due," snarled Masood, red faced.

"So our game is up," suggested Ali."

"Like hell it is," snapped Masood. He was soon on the phone to the Saudi contact.

"Where is the monthly payment?" Masood demanded.

"There has been a delay and it is taking time to calculate the amounts. We do not want to be seen to be trying to cheat you my friend," said Prince Abdulla.

"I am not your friend and if the money is not there as arranged, there will be no further contact," ranted Masood.

"Do not be too hasty, Masood, we are doing our best," replied Prince Abdulla.

"Well it's not good enough. I have told you if the money is not in our account, there will be no code and that means many will die," threatened Masood.

"We will do our best, Inshalla," promised Prince Abdulla.

"Don't give me that. You either do it or boom," said Masood, as he slammed the phone down.

Prince Abdulla was far from happy. He was not used to being spoken to like that, and never by an Indian, who he considered inferior anyway. He was of royal blood and was furious at Masood's words. He could not allow his feelings to get in the way of dealings in this matter. What he had told Masood was partially true. They were having difficulty in calculating the amount each country had to pay, and no one wanted to pay anything, if they could get away with it. The problem was they had no idea where Masood got his information from, and the next bomb could be in their country.

It took many phone calls and lots of reasoning to arrange for the countries to make the transfers required. It was not until the next morning that Masood received the news he had been waiting for.

"They have done it Ali," Masood announced.

"Done what?" asked Ali nervously.

"They have paid the next installment. Over one and a half billion dollars," said Masood, smiling.

"I did not believe they would do it Masood. You are the greatest," laughed Ali, jumping up and down like a monkey.

"Not me. Kutty made all this possible," said Masood.

"I wish you wouldn't keep saying that. It gives me the creeps," confided Ali, calming down.

Cindy came into the lounge from the bedroom.

"Masood, you know I said I was going to arrange for schooling for my Johnny." said Cindy.

"Yes my love," replied Masood.

"Well, I would like to go back home for a week and take care of it. Do you mind?" asked Cindy.

"Of course I mind," Masood replied. "I want you by my side. But you have things to do and you can check on the club while you're there." She planted a big kiss on his upturned lips.

"Thank you for understanding Masood. It means a lot to me," Cindy smiled.

Meanwhile, Mel had taken Ali down to the boat to go for a cruise and try out the bed.

"What about the crew?" asked Ali, as she dragged him into the master suite.

"I can only take one man at a time," joked Mel.

Ali had never made love on silk sheets before and with the motion of the fast moving boat, they slid all over. It added extra spice to their love-making and the thrill of looking up and seeing her man thrusting deep inside her was fantastic. The powerful throb of the engines, along with the regular thump as the boat slid across the tops of the waves, seemed to coincide with his thrusts to bring pleasure she had never known, or even dreamed existed before. It had an effect on Ali too, for his energy seemed to know no bounds, as the boat charged out to sea. She had heard of love-making that was like the crashing of waves, but this was for real and when they came together, she thought the world had ended in a blast of fire. She was in heaven.

They lay there exhausted for a long time before a polite knock on the door brought them back to reality.

"Do you have a destination, Madame," asked the steward through the closed door. "Or shall we turn back?"

I've just reached my destination, Mel thought, as she told him to head back to the marina.

"God Ali, you were fantastic," Mel cooed.

"Not bad yourself," he quipped laughing and rolling off the bed.

She waited while he showered and then showered herself. It was not big enough for them both to get in, a detail she would order to be fixed when they got back.

"That was worth buying the boat for eh Ali?" joked Mel.

"Yes my love. What a ride in more ways than one," he laughed.

"At last," said Saeed gloating. "Due to the stupidity of Beg, we have found where they are staying."

"Yes, but Jaleel has now bought the hotel and they say there are no suites available. Although we can have rooms, they will be spread all over the hotel," complained Khalaf.

"It will not have to matter. We must at least stay within watching distance of them after what happened at Schipol," said Saeed.

He had not enjoyed being made to look a fool in front of all the passengers and his men. He was not a man who forgave easily, and if he ever came across that pilot in different circumstances, he would make him pay.

CHAPTER FIFTEEN
The Gift of Tears

Masood was not at all happy at the prospect of Cindy going away for a week, but he knew she was excited about going home and telling everyone about her new found wealth. Most of all, she was excited at the prospect of seeing her son and her mum, who were flying back to London to meet her.

"I will miss you Cindy," he told her.

"Yes I know, but it will not be for long and then we can spend as much time as you want together. I may bring John back with me for a holiday if that's ok," said Cindy.

"Of course it is. I would be happy for him to join us," said Masood, with just a hint of hesitation in his voice, which did not go unnoticed.

"Now that we have money, it puts us on a better footing, Masood," said Cindy.

"Yes, I suppose it does. You can go out and buy what you like, but Ali and I won't get the pleasure of buying you nice things anymore," complained Masood.

"Nonsense ! You may buy me anything you like at any time. I am always happy for my lover to shower me with presents," Cindy smiled.

They were sitting in their bedroom of the suite, Cindy on the edge of the huge bed, and Masood in a deep comfortable red Moroccan leather armchair. The carpet was thick Wilton in a pale shade of green and the drapes in contrast were pale gold.

"Good, then you won't have any trouble accepting this gift," smiled Masood. He pulled out a large box from a wardrobe, then stepped back and smiled.

"What is it?" Cindy asked.

"Open the box and all will be revealed," Masood urged. She had never had a dress in a box before and she slid off the lid. Filled with excitement and expectation, the contents were covered in red tissue paper, which she quickly discarded, to find another box underneath.

She opened this one to find yellow tissue paper covering the contents, and under that, another box. This went on for several boxes more, and her frustration was visibly mounting when she got to the box of Moroccan tooled leather. She lifted it out of its nest and placed it on the coffee table. Her heart was pounding and she wanted to open the beautiful box, but not daring to for fear of disappointment.

"Open it," came Mel's excited voice from behind her.

Her shaking hands went to the clasp and fumbled with it. A faint click, and it was open. She lifted the lid gently to reveal a necklace of stunning beauty. The emeralds were cut as droplets, starting small at the back and getting progressively larger as they came to the front. They sparkled with green fire reflecting the sunlight in the room onto the ceiling and walls.

"Masood!" she gasped, as she reached to lift the necklace from its velvet bed in the box. As she moved it, the jewels seemed to take on a life of their own, turning the sunlight into green fire, and making it dance across the ceiling and walls. Mel had known Cindy many years and had never seen her cry before, but the beauty of the necklace unlocked the floodgates of years.

Cindy sat and sobbed for a long time, occasionally wiping her eyes to look at the emeralds, but unable to see properly for the veil of tears.

Her mind went back through the years to when she was a little girl of eight, and her father had come home drunk from the pub as usual, but this time he had brought her a gift.

"Cindy," he had roared as he came through the open front door. "Come to daddy. I have a present for you."

She had rushed downstairs to his waiting strong arms. He had picked her up and twirled her around in the stark living room as her mother, Ethel, looked on, afraid he would drop her, but too scared to say anything for fear of another drunken beating. He eventually put her down and reached into his pocket, drawing out a string of red glass beads which sparkled even in the light of the single sixty watt bulb hanging from the ceiling.

"This is for you," he said as he turned her around and fitted them around her neck.

"Oh Dad they're fantastic. I feel like a princess in a film," said Cindy.

"You are a princess," he assured her.

She had worn them to school the next day and her friends were green with envy, but she did not care. She was so proud of them.

It was several days later that her father had brought his friend home for tea, and she met the most horrible man in the world.

"This is Bill. He works with me," announced her dad as they entered the house that evening. She could tell by the look on her mum's face that something was wrong, but she drank her tea and after playing for a while on Bill's knee, she went off to bed.

It was some hours later that she felt someone getting into her bed.

"Shhss Cindy. It's only me Bill."

She often had friends to stay, so someone sharing her bed was not unusual but she didn't like him to keep getting closer. She was afraid and her little heart beat faster and faster. Suddenly the door burst open and her mum ran in.

"Get out," she screamed at Bill.

Startled, Bill leaped out of bed. Cindy had never seen a man naked before, and unknown to her, Bill was in a state of arousal, but not for long. Her mum, without hesitation, kicked him in the groin and he went down like a pole-axe had hit him.

Smack!

The sound of her father hitting her mother again was like a pistol shot, and Cindy dived under the bedcovers.

"Bitch! I'll teach you to hurt my friend," he roared, slapping her again and again, until Cindy could stand it no longer.

"Please daddy. Please," she shouted, scrambling out of bed and trying with all her little might to hold his flailing arms.

Bill was getting dressed, clearly in great pain.

"Leave it Joe," he told her dad. "The bitch has done it for me and I ain't no good now anyway."

The two men stormed from the room and down the stairs whilst her sobbing mother cowered in the corner, blood oozing from a split lip and a cut to her head.

"M…Mum," bleated a tearful Cindy.

"Srroright my petal, honest," reassured her mum, guiding her over to the bed and climbing in next to her, cuddling her as tight as she could.

It was the last of Ethel's many beatings. The next morning she had gone to the police and Joe had been arrested at work, in front of his workmates, along with Bill. They had been charged and bailed, and after a night on the ale, they had made the mistake of turning up for work the next day.

It had been reported as a tragic accident in the local paper, and lots of people had called around to comfort her mum. It was many years later, it had dawned on Cindy, that her dad and Bill didn't work in the part of the factory where they had fallen off the high loading platform onto the railings below.

"What is wrong my love?" asked a concerned Masood interrupting Cindy from her thoughts. "Do you not like green?"

"Noth… nothi… nothing is wrong you wonderful man," Cindy finally managed. "They are so beautiful I could never wear them. I could not do them justice."

"I think you have that the wrong way around Cindy. It is you that is the more beautiful," whispered Masood.

By now, Mel had helped her put them on and she had also fitted the earrings, which Cindy had not noticed when she opened the box. She got up and went over to the mirror, wanting to peep, but feeling apprehensive of how she would look.

One look in the mirror was enough to start the flood of tears again, but not before she had noticed the effect of the green stones in her eyes. She felt like a princess and rushed to Masood to hug him.

"You are the most wonderful man in the world. No one has ever given me a gift before, that didn't have strings attached," Cindy cried.

"Shhh my princess. We will have no talk of the past. This is a new life and we will, with the help of God, enjoy it together. There will be many times like these," promised Masood.

Now, Mel was crying as well.

"Sorry, I didn't get you something Mel," said Ali.

"That's not why I'm crying Ali, you clod. I'm just so happy. Can't a girl cry when she's happy, without a man trying to get in on the act," said Mel.

"Sorry," was Ali's reply.

"Quit while you're ahead Ali," advised Masood.

There was no parting Cindy from her necklace and earrings for the rest of the day. She kept going back to the mirror and admiring them again, and again.

"Ali," shouted Mel.

"Yes."

"I have been thinking of going back to London with Cindy for a few days," Mel continued.

"Oh," he answered, clearly disappointed.

"It won't be for long but there are things I should take care of. We left in such a hurry, I did not have time to say goodbye to anyone properly," Mel explained.

"I am sorry, my love. I forgot you must have family and friends. I am being selfish," apologized Ali.

"Not really. There is only my mum. Dad went off a long time ago with a woman from the local chip shop, and he hasn't been heard of since," said Mel.

"I can't come with you," said Ali.

"No. I don't want you to, not yet. There will be time for you to meet mum and my friends later, but I want to tell them about us on my own first, if you don't mind. It's not because I'm ashamed of you or anything funny, but everything has happened so quickly and I need to get used to it all myself first," said Mel reassuringly.

They had a party that night in the hotel to celebrate Masood buying the hotel, and Mel and Cindy's huge win. It was a party to remember and Cindy took the opportunity to wear her necklace and earrings. Masood made sure the Monte Carlo jet set were invited, and the girls were very excited to rub shoulders with some of the Society of Monte Carlo, including some minor members of the Royal Family.

"You must tell me your system my dear," came a husky voice over Cindy's left shoulder. She turned to find a distinguished looking man with grey hair perfectly combed, a gentle but well tanned face that had seen many years of sun, and the disarming smile of a spider welcoming a fly into its web.

"I was very impressed at your win the other night," said the man.

"Not as impressed as I was," Cindy replied jokingly.

"I am Don Carlos D'Medichi. I have a small interest in the casino my dear. May I refresh your drink?" he offered, stopping a passing waiter before she could reply.

"Thank you that's very kind," said Cindy.

"I am most curious. Why did you bet on number one twice in a row?" asked Don Carlos.

"Oh that! We didn't mean to, we were busy deciding what to do, when the croupier said no more bets," explained Cindy laughing nervously.

"A very lucky accident for you my dear," he replied smiling back at Cindy.

"Yes it was," she answered, looking for anyone she recognized to get away from this sickening man.

"Are you alright?" came another voice from her side, as its owner clasped her arm gently and led her away."

"Thank you. You saved my life," Cindy laughed.

"You're welcome. I am Captain Saeed Alman." He was dark and handsome with a charming smile. "I am from Iran. That is a beautiful necklace you're wearing. It matches your lovely eyes, if I may say so."

"Thank you," said Cindy blushing.

"Would you care to dance?" asked Saeed.

She accepted without hesitation, and he guided her to the ballroom. He was light on his feet and a good dancer.

"Are you on holiday or on business?" Saeed inquired, making polite conversation, but already knowing the answers.

"I came with some friends for a holiday," Cindy answered.

"How long will you stay?" Saeed asked.

"I am returning to London tomorrow," she replied. This was not the answer he had expected.

"Why, do you not like it here?" he asked.

"No, it's lovely. But I have to go to see my son and my mother," replied Cindy. Now he was getting somewhere. So she had family and this could provide leverage in the future, and was valuable information. He was very glad he had rescued her from "Mr Slimy" of the casino.

"Thank you for rescuing me from that awful man," said Cindy.

"Yes he was. You looked mortified," laughed Saeed.

"I was. I felt him undressing me with his eyes all the time," replied Cindy.

"Yes. I think he would have liked to have done that, had he gotten the chance," Saeed laughed again.

"Ugh. What an awful thought," was her reply. They finished their dance, and headed for the bar, where they had a drink and chatted for a while. Then she spotted Ali and excused herself.

"Ali. All the men here are creeps. All of them are after getting their hands on your money, or getting in your knickers. I don't know which is worse," complained Cindy.

"Oh, them getting in your knickers," Ali joked, which cheered her up no end.

Masood was enjoying the party and making some good contacts for investment when Cindy found him.

"May we go Masood? It's our last night together for a bit, and I want to spend some of it by ourselves," Cindy pleaded, batting her come-to-bed eyes at him.

"Of course we can, my love. Anything you want," said Masood.

"And I haven't thanked you properly for my present," she winked. He smacked his lips in anticipation as they left the party, and went up to the suite. Mel was glued to Ali's side for the rest of the evening. She was leaving him for a few days and was already regretting her decision to go.

"Of course you must go, lover. It is only a few days and you cannot let your mother down now," reassured Ali.

"When I get back, the changes to the boat will be done and I will take you out for a cruise. I will make it up to you Ali, I promise," purred Mel.

"What more can a man ask than that?" he replied. Neither of them was to know that fate had other plans in store for them.

"Now that I have you to myself Masood, what can I do to thank you for the fantastic present you gave me today, and to punish you for making me undo all those boxes to get to the real thing?" asked Cindy, grinning.

"I don't know, my love, but I'm sure you will think of something. Don't forget the threats you made in Dubai, before Ali was bitten. You never made good on them," laughed Masood.

"Sounds like I will need all night to sort this out lover," purred Cindy. She rang room service and ordered champagne and sandwiches.

"And don't forget to send salt and pepper with them," Cindy ordered.

"Why do you want food, my love? Are you hungry?" asked a confused Masood.

"You will find out. Now get those clothes off and run the bath and make sure it's hot," she ordered.

"Yes my love," answered Masood. He scuttled off to the bathroom and emerged twenty minutes later wearing just a big grin. "Ready my love," he announced to Cindy, and the blushing waitress who had just arrived with the tray Cindy had ordered.

Cindy burst out laughing, lightening the moment, while the blushing waitress turned and ran for the door stifling her own laughter as she exited. His erection was the only part of Masood that wasn't bright red.

"Another debt to be paid," was all Cindy said, before collapsing on the bed doubled up laughing.

"Sorry," said Masood.

"Don't apologize. Just get in the bath you clown," ordered Cindy.

"Ouch! It's too hot," screeched Masood. He was stepping out when she grabbed him.

"Get in, you bloody softie," she ordered.

"But I feel like a lobster," complained Masood.

"You can eat later. All you ever think of is eating," laughed Cindy relishing the moment.

"No. I mean I feel as if I am going to be cooked like a lobster," explained Masood.

"Then perhaps you won't be so cruel to them in the future," she answered, pushing him down into the hot water. She got a new bar of soap from a bag she had in the bathroom, and started to bathe him as he lay in the hot water.

"Ouch! What are you using on me?" he asked.

"Oh, it's a bar of soap that I rubbed some sand into for just such an occasion as this," said Cindy smiling.

He grinned. "I knew you would think of something," he gloated. By the time he got out of the bath, he was covered in angry scratches.

"You go and lie on the bed now lover. I will be with you in a minute," Cindy cooed.

"Yes my love," he said complying.

"Are you face down?" demanded Cindy.

"Yes my love," answered Masood.

"No peeking, or you won't get the treat I have planned for you," cooed Cindy.

"I'm face down, honest," came the muffled reply.

Standing on the bed towering over him, she began to sprinkle the contents of the salt and pepper cellars all over him.

"Aaargh!" he cried squirming.

"Keep still you baby," Cindy ordered, kicking him at the same time. He was squirming around now loving every minute of it. She knew he was in heaven and later he would take her there too.

CHAPTER SIXTEEN
Reunion in London

When they headed for the airport the next day, they were followed by Saeed and his men. It had been decided that Asif and Omar would follow the girls back to London, and see what they could learn of their lives, while the rest stayed with Masood and Ali.

It was a tearful farewell at the airport, but they all agreed it would not be long before they were back together. If Masood and Ali had to move on, it was arranged that they would leave messages with Bernard, the hotel manager, for Cindy and Mel. It was a quiet Ali and Masood who ate dinner that night in the hotel.

Cindy and Mel chattered all the way back to London, and when they emerged from the arrivals area, both were welcomed by two excited mums and Cindy's son. Many hugs and kisses later, Mel was first to speak.

"Oh mum he is fantastic. He is the kindest man in the world and so gentle." She proudly showed them all a photo of Ali.

"I hope you don't mind that he's Indian," said Mel nervously.

"I don't care if he's from the moon as long as he makes my little girl happy. If not, I'll cut his tackle off and make no mistake," cackled Mel's mum.

"You'll…" Mel stopped mid word.

"What did you say love?" her mum asked.

"Nothing, just thinking out loud," Mel answered.

Need a big knife, she finished the sentence off in her head and laughed.

"So, what is your man like then Cindy?" asked Ethel, her mum.

"Just right for me," came Cindy's reply, her thoughts miles away on a foreign shore.

"I want to know more than that my girl," demanded Ethel.

"Yes mum. What's he like. Come on, tell us," pleaded Johnny.

"He is generous and funny and thoughtful, and good to me ma. Is that enough?" answered Cindy.

"And where did you two find these two saints then? A Christmas cracker?" asked Mel's mum.

"No, they came in the club one night," defended Mel.

"Not such angels then are they?" inquired her mum.

"Never said they were," snapped Mel. "I just said they were good to us, and anyway they gave us the club so we didn't have to depend on them for any money. Now that we've won all this money at the casino, we are free to do what we want. There will be no more working at the club, even if we finish with Ali or Masood."

"Anyway…" jumped in Cindy "…we haven't come home for an argument. We came home to tell you what has happened and hope that you're happy for us."

"'Course we're happy for you Cindy," said Ethel. "How could we not be?"

They were in the taxi now on the way into London. Mary, Mel's mum, was wearing her best coat, a camel coloured three-quarter length one. Mel had bought her this the last time they had gone shopping together. She had thought it was too young for her, but she loved it now and it was warm as well.

Ethel, having just come back from Spain, was wearing a floral print summer dress, pale blue with yellow flowers, and yellow shoes to match.

"How are you doing at school Johnny? Are you still having problems with bullying?" asked Cindy.

"Na, not no longer," replied Johnny.

"Don't you lie to me, or it will be a tanning when we get home and that's for sure," challenged Cindy.

"Leave the lad alone. You just got here and you're picking on him already," defended Ethel.

They chatted for the rest of the journey into London, and then parted at Mary's flat close to Dartford Tunnel.

"See you at the club tomorrow night love," Cindy called, as the taxi drew away and into the traffic.

Mel didn't get any sleep that night, as she told her mum all about Ali, their meeting, his near-death experience in Dubai, and his reaction to her acceptance to marry him.

"He never run through one of them posh hotels naked?" said Mary, amazed by all that had happened.

"Yes he did," laughed Mel.

"Did they throw him out?" Mary asked.

"No mum. They tried, but Masood bought the hotel," replied Mel grinning.

"Now I know you're winding me up girl. No one could do that," Mary questioned.

"It's true mum. I was there when Masood sacked the general manager for trying to have us all thrown out because of what Ali did. It was ever so funny," giggled Mel.

"Well I never. He must be made of money."

"He is mum. He is."

"So, is your Ali a flunky for Masood then?

"No mum they are equal partners."

It was breakfast time when they realized how tired they were, and the excitement had died down.

"I'll rustle up some breakfast and then you'd better get some sleep my girl," Mary advised. Mel wolfed the full cooked breakfast down, and after a hot bath, went to bed. She was asleep as soon as her head hit the pillow.

Cindy had a similar night with her mum, with Johnny pleading to stay up so he could hear all the exciting bits. They carried him up to bed at about 3:00 am, and lasted, themselves, until around 5:00 am.

Mel and Cindy met up at the club that evening for a report from Jim.

"The Club's not doing so well since you two left," complained Jim. He went through the pretence of showing them the books he had made up, and they let him think they believed his story. They left after a few hours, before the club was due to get busy, and Jim was glad to see them go.

"Do you believe that bastard trying to get one over on us?" asked Cindy.

"No, I think we should have an investigator watch the Club and see what he reports," suggested Mel.

"I have a better idea," said Cindy. "It's cheaper to ask Jill. She was always a good friend and I saw her in there tonight with the Judge so we can wait till she goes home and have a chat."

They made themselves comfortable in a nearby coffee bar and waited. At about 2:00 am, Jill came out with a client in tow.

"Mel!! How are you? Cindy!" shouted Jill.

"Oh a threesome," piped up the client.

"Get lost creep," said Jill shoving him away. He stumbled off down the street grumbling something about tarts.

"Heard about your win, lucky bitches," joked Jill.

"How?" asked Mel.

"You were in the papers, love. All over page one," explained Jill smiling.

"That's an improvement on page three," quipped Cindy. "Where shall we go?" they all asked at the same time.

"The Dorchester," replied Mel.

On arrival, they were greeted with strange looks by the night receptionist, who kept looking up from the form with questioning glances.

"Excuse me ladies, but you seem familiar and yet I am sure we have never met," said the receptionist.

"You're right mate. You haven't met my friends, but you seen them in the papers this week," quipped Jill.

"Page one, on Monday! You won all that money at the casino," replied the receptionist. He quickly checked them in and they were shown up to the suite in minutes.

"Fame has its advantages," joked Jill. They sent for drinks and settled down to a good gossip.

"So the bastard has been making a fortune has he?" remarked Cindy.

"In my opinion, he has, love. Since you went, there's more water in the drinks and the prices have gone up. He takes more off the girls and says it's your instructions," explained Jill. She was all for leaving after breakfast, but they persuaded her to stay and sleep the drink off with them.

"Hello girls," said a nervous Jim as they returned to the club with Jill that night.

"Come back again to see how badly we're doing? Suppose it was hard to believe what I told you last night?" he asked.

"In a way Jim, we have. You see, we've been having a little chat with Jill and it seems you weren't quite truthful last night. Before the punters start coming in, we want a word with the girls," said Cindy, in a tone that sent a shiver down Jim's spine. Jill had already rounded everyone up, including the girls not on duty that night, and the sight of all the girls made Jim very nervous.

"Now Jim, we know you've been screwing the girls money-wise, and us, and the punters on the drinks, so Mel and I are going to change things. We've seen a lawyer today and the club now belongs jointly to the girls. It's up to them what they do with it now, and with you," said Cindy eyes gleaming.

Jim was dumfounded, and on looking around, found all the girls were smiling at him.

"Then I suppose I'm sacked," he shrugged and turned to leave, only to find three huge men, who he had never seen before, standing between him and the door.

"Yes Jim, you're fired, and these three gentlemen will show you the way out, and take you home. We believe the girls have a leaving present for you before you go. You could call it a golden boot," Cindy smiled.

They stripped Jim first, then the three men held him while in order of longest serving, the girls were allowed a kick each, wherever they wanted. Even the hard men holding him winced as a girl's stiletto shoe's struck Jim's groin area again, and again. It was doubtful Jim ever bothered a woman again, or fathered any children. He was found adorning a local pawn broker's sign from which two of the balls had been removed so Jim's could replace them. His swollen glands had been helpfully painted brass coloured to match the original ones. It is rumoured the local protection collectors don't collect from the club any more.

There was a party at the club that night and the customers were locked out. Cindy, Mel, and the girls drank the place dry. It was certainly a party to remember.

Free from business, Cindy set out to find a school for Johnny to go to.

Meanwhile, Mel had decided to buy her mum a house.

"You can't go doing that with your money, love. It won't last you long at this rate," cautioned Mary.

"Mum, you have looked after me and now I want to spend a bit on you. What's wrong with that?" asked Mel.

"Nothing, but it's such a lot of money and I like my flat," argued Mary.

"No you don't. You've been saying for years you wanted the council to move you and they wouldn't. The damp in your bedroom isn't doing your health any good is it? So look on me as the council. I won't take no for an answer and I have arranged for us to go and look at some houses today. If you don't like those, we can keep looking until we find one you do like," assured Mel.

It took a few days, but they found a lovely house in Hampstead Heath.

"Are you sure about this, love? It is a lot of money and I don't need all that room, just for me," said Mary.

"Course I'm sure. It means a lot to me mum and it is a beautiful house. I will see the agents today and get you moved in before I go back to Ali," promised Mel.

Although it would delay her return, Ali was fine about it when she called him to tell him the news.

"It will mean by the time I get the flight to come back to you, my mum will be in her new home. She is trying not to show it, but she is so excited," said Mel, the excitement so clear in her voice; it brought a lump to Ali's throat.

"Yes my love. I can hear the excitement in your voice. Have a nice time and I will see you in a few more days," assured Ali.

After ending her call to Ali, Mel went to the estate agent's office.

"Good morning Miss Mountjoy. Nice to see you again," greeted the estate agent as Mel entered the office. "How can I help?"

"I would like to put an offer in on the property in Hampstead Heath," Mel answered.

His eyes lit up.

"Good, I will get the file," replied the estate agent. He was gone only a minute and returned with an expectant smile on his face. "And what figure did you have in mind? We have had plenty of interest in this house."

"Please! Save the sales talk," Mel chided. "Two hundred thousand pounds."

"There must be some mistake. The asking price is one hundred and sixty five thousand pounds," he said looking visibly shocked.

"Yes, I am aware of that but there are two conditions to my offer. First, my mum must not be told how much I paid for it, because she is very proud of being working class. Second, she wants to move in on Friday," replied Mel smiling.

"Bu… but that's impossible!" stuttered the agent.

"Oh well, if that's the case I will find another house," said Mel heading for the door.

"No please wait. I must call the vendors and see what I can do, but I would be surprised if it can be done," said the agent excusing himself so he could call the vendors. He went into the back office and she made herself comfortable while she waited. It was half an hour before he returned.

"I have good news, Miss Mountjoy. The vendors have agreed to your offer and the deadline you asked for."

"I rather thought they would," replied Mel. "These are my details and the solicitor is expecting the papers ASAP. Remember, if it's not signed and sealed by Thursday, the deal is off," said Mel. She left and got a taxi back to her mum's flat, asking the driver to wait while she got her mum.

"Come on mum, we are going to look at your new house," urged Mel.

"But I'm in me apron, girl."

"Who cares? Just put your coat on and let's get going. I have a cab waiting downstairs," urged Mel.

Mary went into her bedroom. Mel was right, the place was a dump. She had been there since the war and the estate was rough enough then, but now there was always trouble and fights. The gangs of young thugs ran the streets and the police stayed away. The council workers never came to do any repairs because they were too afraid of the gangs. It was so long since her flat had been decorated, she had forgotten when it was last done.

With her coat on, she closed the bedroom door and joined Mel in the lounge, tears in her eyes.

"Come on mum. It will be fine and your new house will be better and safer than here," Mel assured her, closing her hand on Mary's arm.

They closed the door to the flat and, going over to the lift, pressed the button to go down. The doors opened and they got in, pressing the button for the ground floor. The lift smelled of urine and the walls were covered in graffiti, and stickers advertising local prostitutes' descriptions and telephone numbers.

As they got out of the lift, the two youths lounging by the front door came over.

"Got any money on you darling?" demanded the shorter of the two lads.

"No I haven't. Now sod off," replied Mel.

"No need to be rude. Maybe a kiss would pay your exit fee," said the taller of the two, leering at them and making Mel feel like being sick. They were both about eighteen to twenty, with greasy slicked back hair, black leather jackets, and trouble written all over them.

"Come on darling, a quickie in the lift for each of us," said the shorter of the two, his face was pockmarked. He hadn't shaved for a while and his breath was putrid. "And you and grandma can be on your way. Don't want to get rough now, do we?"

"Think you're a regular hard-case do you?" challenged Mel, hoping someone would come, or that the taxi driver would come looking for her.

"Hard enough darling? Hard enough," sneered the shorter lad again.

Crrrunch was the noise shorty's face made as it hit the concrete pillar, blood spurting from his smashed nose.

Startled by the noise and sight, Mel and Mary turned to see the smiling face of Asif.

"No respect for ladies these days," said Asif, casually letting the lad's head go as he slid to the floor. By this time, the second youth's knife was heading for Asif's back. Mel's cry of warning stuck in her throat, as in a blur of movement, Asif, avoided the stabbing blow, and spun and grabbed the lad's arm. A loud cracking noise announced the breaking of the lad's elbow joined by a scream of agony from his mouth. Arrgggggg was all the lad got out before Asif wrenched the shattered joint apart, then let the lad's arm fall useless and dangling. A kick to the back of the lad's left knee as his momentum made him stagger past Asif, shattered the knee as well, leaving him helpless on the floor screaming in agony.

"Thanks," was all a shaken Mel managed to say before Asif was gone.

"Bloody hell love, who was he?" asked Mary.

"Oh, one of Masood's bodyguards," Mel mumbled, Just as confused as Mary.

Still a bit shaken, they walked to the waiting taxi and got in. Thankful to be off the street, they went to look at the house.

"He must be bloody loaded to need bodyguards, love," said a shaken Mary.

"He is mum, he is. If you had any doubt before, what just happened is even more reason for you to move eh mum?" urged Mel.

"Yes love, you're right I know you're right."

CHAPTER SEVENTEEN
Toys for the Boys

"So, what shall we do while the girls are away?" asked Ali.

"I think I am going to buy a jet, Ali," replied Masood.

Spppfffff Ali's coffee went everywhere as he nearly choked, and tried to stop from dropping his cup.

"Now I know you're mad, Masood. They cost a lot of money," said Ali, recovering from what Masood had just said.

"Ali, oh Ali my friend, you still have not got it have you. We can have anything money can buy."

"Yes but…"

"Do not but me, Ali," Masood's raised voice challenged. "I am the business brain and you are not, and if I want to buy a plane out of my half, I will damn well buy one."

"Yes, Masood, if you say so," Ali replied, totally taken aback by the tone of his friend's voice.

"I do Ali, I do."

Unknown to Ali, Masood had already contacted an aircraft dealer who was on his way from Geneva as they spoke. The hotel limo collected him from the airport and brought him to the hotel, where he was shown to his room, and his arrival conveyed to Masood. They met that evening at dinner in Masood's suite.

"Good evening, Mr Jaleel, a pleasure to meet you."

"Good evening, Mr Greenberg, the pleasure is all mine. This is my associate, Mr Beg." Aperitifs were ordered while they exchanged small talk.

"Did you have any particular aircraft in mind, Mr Jaleel?" asked Greenberg.

"Masood, Please call me Masood. No. I have no firm type in mind. Cost is not an object, but it must be fitted out to the highest standard and have two bedrooms."

"I have brought with me photographs of some of the conversions my company has done. I am, for obvious reasons, unable to give you a client list, but it will give you some idea of what can be achieved," continued Greenberg.

The food arrived, and they ate and talked for over three hours.

"We have covered a lot of ground in a few hours and I would like to suggest a trip to one of our workshop hangers in Hamburg. Would tomorrow be convenient?"

"It would, Mr Greenberg," confirmed Masood without referring to Ali.

"In that case, I will bid you goodnight, as I have some arrangements to make before I settle down for the night."

"This is very exciting. You are so clever but we must be due to get another letter soon and have to move on," warned Ali.

"Yes. I think one is due tomorrow, but I have a plan for staying here until the girls get back, without messing up Kutty's arrangements," assured Masood.

It was very early morning when Ali visited Masood's room. He was only there a few minutes and returned to his room.

They were both right and the following morning a letter arrived for Masood. As the girls weren't around, Masood opened it in the room.

"We're to go to Stockholm Ali."

"But I thought we were going to Hamburg," said Ali confused.

"We are. I can take care of what I have to do here, and then we can meet Mr Greenberg, and fly to Hamburg. After that, we can go to Stockholm and still be back here for when the girls get back." It did not take Masood long to get his message through, and after breakfast, they left with Greenberg for the airport.

"I have one of our private jets waiting, Masood, so that it will give you some idea of what we do," said Greenberg.

The jet was a Lear, which is all Masood remembered. He was more interested in the interior than the technical specifications. Greenberg soon realized this, and concentrated on the sumptuous interior of the aircraft. Ali thought the stewardess was sumptuous too. It was a good job Mel was not around. It was whisper-quiet in the aircraft and they had no trouble hearing Greenberg as he went through his sales pitch.

"I have been thinking over what you said last night Masood, and it occurs to me that, while this is a beautiful aircraft, it will not be large enough for the way you have indicated you would like it fitted out," said Greenberg.

"Do you have a larger aircraft in mind Mr Greenberg?" asked Masood.

Greenberg looked thoughtful.

"I do Masood. We have a 707 available at the moment, which would certainly meet all your requirements with some space to spare. It would not be too difficult to convert as we had already started it for a South American dictator, who has since been deposed and has no use for it," explained Greenberg.

"Excellent, Mr Greenberg, excellent," smiled Masood.

Masood sat back, and sipped his drink with a sense of great satisfaction. He thought he had a good life with his recruitment agency, but nothing like this, and he loved every minute of it. He was deep in thought when the stewardess leaned towards him.

"We're coming in to land. Sir, please fasten your seat belt," she whispered.

Her blouse fell downwards revealing a wonderful cleavage and she did not miss him noticing, ensuring she stayed leaning over long enough for him to get a good eyeful, but not too long to make it obvious.

The landing was very smooth and they taxied to the hanger to disembark, where they were met by Greenberg's project manager.

"Hello Otto. I have been explaining to Masood about the 707 and he would like to see it if possible," asked Greenberg.

"It is out on the field, mothballed, but if you don't mind some dust, I can have it ready for inspection after lunch," confirmed Otto.

"Excellent," replied Masood. Before going for lunch, they were shown around two of the hangers in which aircraft were in various stages of conversion.

"This is very interesting Mr Greenberg. I had not realized you could do so much, or get so much into an aircraft before," said Masood.

"It is a matter of good design and we have the best designers in the world. We are not the cheapest, but we use only the best material and craftsmen. We will not rush. The company motto translates, "if we do it right, we do it our way."

"I like that very much. What do you think Ali?"

"Oh, yes Masood," Ali replied not really knowing what they were talking about. He was too busy wishing he was with Mel now. He missed her more than he thought he would and wanted her back in the hotel suite on the big bed, making love in ways only she knew how.

"What do you think Hans?" asked Helga, the stewardess with the large cleavage.

Hans was the pilot of the jet that had brought Masood and Ali to Hamburg.

"They must be very rich. I heard the man Masood, say to that fat slime Greenberg, that money was no object," said Helga.

"Yes Helga. They seem to be loaded and we could get a good ransom for them. I will make some calls and see what can be arranged. It is short notice, but we need funds and we have to take our chances when we can." They were both members of Bader Meinhoff, a lethal German terrorist organisation.

After lunch, Masood and Ali went over to the Boeing 707 which had now, to some extent, been prepared for them. It was a large aircraft and, for maximum effect, it had been arranged for them to enter at the front.

"This is huge, Mr Greenberg. Are you sure I need something this big?" asked Masood.

"It is, of course, up to you, but taking into account your wish list which will take up a lot of space, you don't want to be cramped do you?" asked Greenberg. He was a good salesman and knew which buttons to press with men like Masood. Anyway, he had been trying to offload this aircraft for some time, and was not going to let this chance slip away.

"No, no. I want plenty of room," confirmed Masood.

Otto took over from here on the tour.

"You have asked for two large bedrooms with shower rooms for each. I suggest they occupy opposite ends of the aircraft. Do you want a large lounge area in the middle with a bar, or two separate lounge areas, Mr Masood?" asked Otto.

"What do you think Ali? One large lounge sounds best to me." said Masood.

"Yes. I agree. It will be nicer if we all relax and fly together. The bar is a great idea," said Ali.

"Then it is settled. One lounge it is," confirmed Masood, smiling.

"I assume you want an office area with the latest communication?" asked Otto.

"Yes," confirmed Masood.

"Can we have larger windows?" asked Ali.

"Afraid not Sir," replied Otto, hiding his amusement. They are part of the structure of the aircraft. We can do lots of things except change the structural integrity of the aircraft."

They spent the rest of the afternoon choosing materials and fittings. Masood found it hard to contain his excitement.

"I will work out the costing, Masood, and bring them to your hotel in the morning when I call to fly you back to Monte Carlo. We would like you to be our guests for the evening," invited Greenberg.

"That's very nice of you, Mr Greenberg. We accept," said Masood, without conferring with Ali.

A limo took them into Hamburg and left them at the city's best hotel. Greenberg would be joining them later for dinner.

"Do you think we could go to one of their Bier Kellers, Masood? I have always wanted to go to one," said Ali rather excitedly.

"I am sure it can be arranged," Masood replied, wanting to please his friend.

At eight, there was a knock on the door, and Masood answered it.

"Good evening. Masood. I have reserved a table and have some friends in the restaurant waiting to meet you both," greeted Greenberg.

"Lead on, Greenberg. We are hungry." On arrival, Greenberg introduced his wife.

"This is Heidi, my wife," he announced proudly. She was a little fat lady, with short blonde hair, and a beaming smile which showed off her two gold teeth. Her stubby arm reached forward and she shook Masood's hand. He noticed how small her hands were.

"Pleased to meet you," Heidi nodded and shook Ali's hand as well.

Also in the group, was a middle aged couple. There were also two young women who, from the way they were dressed, left little to the imagination of their purpose for the evening.

Ali thought he recognized one of the ladies. She was a busty blonde, with an hourglass figure. It was the figure he was sure of, but not too sure of her face.

"Have we met before?" Ali asked, a little embarrassed.

"Yes, we met on the flight today. My name is Helga. I was your..."

"Stewardess," he finished the sentence for her.

Greenberg was an astute people person, and had noticed on the flight, that Ali had not taken his eyes off Helga. Masood was not so easy to judge, so Greenberg had brought along Chantelle, a tall, brunette whose tight outfit made the most of her slim figure. Her skirt was split up both sides from hem to thigh, revealing shapely legs. She had long dark hair nearly down to her waspish waist, and sparkling blue eyes. Even with all this, in Masood's eyes, she was no match for Cindy.

Greenberg had arranged the seating to ensure the women sat to the left of Masood and Ali. As they ate and drank, Helga's hand slipped under the table, and gently worked its wicked way along Ali's thigh until reaching his, by now, bulging crotch. It was all she could do not to gasp as she found his enlarged member. Ali found it impossible not to smile. Yes, he thought, that must have been a shock, my dear. She had turned him on, but he had no intention of anything happening. He was not prepared to risk losing Mel over a one night stand.

After the meal, Greenberg, hearing of Ali's wish, suggested they go to a local Bier Keller where there was also a cabaret.

"Excellent eh Ali? Excellent," said Masood.

"Yes Masood," agreed Ali, smiling.

Ali had difficulty leaving the restaurant without everyone noticing his erection. He walked as closely to Helga as he could, but this only made it look like he wanted her there and then.

"Ali likes Helga," Greenberg remarked.

"I think that is obvious, but she is in for a shock if she gets his pants off. He is massive," said Masood.

"Yes. I think everyone in the restaurant noticed that," replied Greenberg.

The Bier Keller was busy with a very smoky atmosphere. Somehow, Greenberg found a table for them and they were soon seated and drinking from large steins of frothy beer. It wasn't too long before Helga had Ali up on the small dance floor, shuffling around.

"You're a big boy Ali," smiled Helga.

"Yes," he replied, a little embarrassed.

"I bet all the girls love you," she said, slipping her hand down between them, and giving him a gentle squeeze. He went red enough to light up the room and this made her smile even more.

When we kidnap you, I am going to have some private fun before we give you back, she thought. All she could think of as they danced was having him inside her, and it was almost too much to bear.

Ali, for his part, was enjoying the closeness of her body as it rubbed against him, occasionally punctuated by her playfully squeezing him. She could not wait until the end of the night. She wanted that monster in her now.

"Ali, I need some fresh air. The smoke in here is hurting my eyes. Can we go out into the garden for a while?" asked Helga.

"Yes. It is getting in my eyes as well," he answered. She led him out to the garden at the rear of the building and they stood and looked at the stars for a few minutes. He felt his zip being undone and reached to stop her.

"No Helga," Ali protested. But she was quick and down on her knees tasting him already. She was hungry as well, for he had never seen anyone take so much of him. She must surely choke any second now, but she knew what she was doing and was enjoying herself.

He tried to stop himself but she was determined, and he exploded, still inside her mouth. She drank it all savouring every drop.

"That wasn't meant to happen," he protested.

"It may not have been in your plan, but it was certainly in mine," Helga replied, rising from her knees, and licking her full red lips.

"You can show me your appreciation later," she winked, taking him by the hand and leading him back to the table.

"Looks like Ali had a good time," remarked Greenberg to Masood.

"Yes, but he will feel guilty later. I know he will," remarked Masood.

Everyone enjoyed the evening and at the end, they left in separate taxis. Ali, Masood, Helga and Chantelle were in one taxi and Greenberg's party in another.

"I will call for you in the morning. Oh, it is morning. Call for you about ten, Masood!" shouted Greenberg as the taxi pulled away.

"Yes, that's fine.See you later," answered Masood.

At the hotel, the ladies got out of the cab as well.

"Sorry girls. It's been a busy day and we have another tomorrow," said Masood, to Ali's relief. "Thanks for the offer, but another time." Helga and Chantelle were confused, and a little annoyed, but they had no choice but to get back into the cab and go home.

"Thanks for that Masood," said Ali, very relieved.

"You're welcome. I know she cornered you at the Bier Keller, but thought you wouldn't want to let Mel down, and I certainly don't want anyone but Cindy," said Masood.

"You won't tell Mel, will you?" asked Ali.

"No, I won't my friend. It's up to you if you tell her or not," answered Masood.

"Where the hell have they gone now?" demanded Saeed.

"I don't know. They went to the airport and boarded a small jet and now they have disappeared," answered a sickly-looking Yousef.

"That's not good enough. You and Riad were supposed to be watching them and you've lost them you idiots," ranted Saeed.

"We could do nothing. They got on a private jet and were gone. What should we have done, followed them in our car?" Yousef ended sarcastically.

"Never mind the sarcasm. We have to find them. What was the range of those things Swami put in Masood's shoes?" demanded Saeed.

"About one hundred miles," answered Riad. "As long as the flash bastard was wearing a pair we bugged, and not another new pair."

"Don't even think like that. It's too horrible to contemplate," Saeed shuddered. He could feel that posting to the Iran/Iraq border calling his name. It took some time to charter a private jet through the Embassy, and a lot of explaining to Abdul Aziz.

"Find them at any cost, you miserable son of a pig," was Aziz's last comment before he slammed the phone down. Aziz was furious and he began to wonder if Saeed had been a good choice to lead the mission.

It took a substantial amount of string-pulling and favour-calling to find out the flight plan of Greenberg's aircraft and its final destination. They were not to know that by the time they were on their way to Hamburg, Masood and Ali were on the way back.

"Seven million dollars is a lot of money," said Ali.

"I wish I hadn't told you now," retorted Masood. You will go on about it forever won't you?"

"No. It's your money and you can do what you want with it," said Ali. Helga was serving them drinks and giving Ali the eye, but he was embarrassed about the previous evening, and trying to avoid her glances.

"Have I done something to offend you?" she whispered, as she bent over with his drink.

"No, no," replied Ali, nervously. "I just have a lot on my mind," he spluttered.

CHAPTER EIGHTEEN
The Libyan Effect

"At last, we have the order we have been waiting for," whooped Kaleel, replacing the telephone handset. Of the two Libyans, he was the most excitable.

"We can go after those two bitches that were with Jaleel and Beg and get some information out of them, and have some fun at the same time," said Kaleel. His mouth was watering at the prospect and it was dribbling down his chin.

Kaleel had just finished talking to their boss in Tripoli.

"Are you sure they are on their own?" asked Ahmed, head of the security services in Libya.

"Yes, we have followed them here from Monte Carlo, and for two days now, all they have done is visit the nightclub they used to work in and go to some relatives' flats. They were met at the airport by two old ladies and a little boy."

"It just gets better all the time," sneered Ahmed. "We may have use of the lad and the old ladies, if you can't get the women to talk, but for now I want you to get the women and make them talk. I don't care what you have to do to get them talking. Am I making myself clear?"

"Yes, Ahmed. Yes," drooled Kaleel. He had dreamed of this day for weeks and he was going to make the most of it.

"Good. Then get on with it and call me as soon as you have news," ordered Ahmed.

Kaleel was glad they had chosen to follow Mel and Cindy back to London. He was convinced that the girls were the key to getting information.

Mel had just left the solicitor's office after handing over the banker's draft and signing the documents for the purchase of the house for her mum. She was so pleased with herself, she would not have noticed her followers if they had been right behind her. She was meeting up with Cindy and they were going shopping for presents for Masood and Ali. Cindy was already at the coffee shop when Mel arrived.

"Hi doll," she greeted Mel like a long lost sister. "Do you want a coffee or shall we go now?"

"Let's go now. I can hardly wait to get to Bond Street. I hope they haven't sold what I have in mind for Ali. What are you getting Masood?" asked Mel.

"A sharp knife to cut his wotsit off if he hasn't behaved himself," joked Cindy. They left the coffee shop and linked arms as they walked down the street, totally unaware of their unwanted escorts thirty metres behind.

It was not long before they were on Bond Street and inside the book and ephemera shop that Mel had been going on about.

"May I help you ladies?" asked the bespectacled man behind the counter. He seemed very, very, old with just a wisp or two if silver hair, trying in vain to cover his shiny head. His moustache was nicotine-stained and there were several food stains on his frayed, worn shirt.

"Yes please," said Mel. "You had a card in here the other day. It was in that case," she said, looking disappointedly at the now empty space which the little card had occupied. "It's not there. Have you sold it?" she asked, with just a hint of hope in her voice.

The shop was poorly lit and it was difficult to see the items which were on sale.

"No Madam. You're in luck. A gentleman wanted to look at it yesterday and I forgot to put it back," apologized the elderly shopkeeper. "Now where did I put it?" he asked himself. Looking forlornly at the shelves behind him, he searched for a few more minutes as they waited impatiently. "Ah yes, here it is. Charles Dickens. Is that the one?"

"Yes! Yes!" Mel blurted. She was so excited; she nearly snatched it from his hand. She was reaching eagerly for it when he stopped her.

"Sorry Madam, but I must ask you to wear these special gloves. The chemicals from your fingers can damage an old card like this." He handed her a pair of white cotton gloves and gave a pair to Cindy as well.

"Isn't it the most amazing thing you have ever seen Cindy?" Mel asked, gazing lovingly at the small buff coloured card in her hand.

"Not sure doll. You haven't let me look at it yet," remarked Cindy with a hint of sarcasm.

"Oh sorry," said Mel, handing the little card to Cindy.

"What is it?" asked Cindy not at all interested in the little card and impatient to get out of the little shop and into the clothes shops.

"Why, it's a business card of Mr Charles Dickens, Madam," replied the shopkeeper in a tone of disapproval. "You know who he was don't you?" he asked.

"Course I do. Think I'm ignorant or something?" snapped Cindy.

"How much is it?" asked Mel, trying to take the heat out of the situation.

"Ten thousand pounds, Madam," puffed the shopkeeper.

"Fucking hell! It's not made of gold is it?" interrupted Cindy. She was quickly working out how many new outfits she could buy for that amount.

"No Madam, but it may as well be. It's very rare indeed," replied the shopkeeper.

"Don't be daft. He must have made lots of cards," argued Cindy who was getting bored with all this fuss over a bit of card.

"Yes he did, but all the ones that are around are from after he became famous, and he signed them all. This one was while he was a shorthand writer, and before he became famous, so it's not signed. That's what makes it so special," explained the old man.

"So you're saying this is the only one of these in the world?" asked Cindy, suddenly interested in the little card.

"S..right," confirmed the shopkeeper smiling.

"I don't care if it is or not, I want it anyway for my Ali," said Mel.

"He's keen on Charles Dickens then, Madam?" the old man asked.

"Yes. He's his favourite author," Mel replied proudly.

"How do you wish to pay for it?"

"Will cash be ok?" Mel asked, reaching into her handbag and pulling out a large wad of fifty pound notes.

"Are you bloody mad Mel carrying that around with you?" demanded Cindy. "Bloody money's gone to your head girl."

"It's ok. We have our escorts outside. They were sent by Ali so no one will harm us will they?" protested Mel.

"What fucking escorts?" demanded Cindy, rushing to the shop window to look outside.

"The two men in front of the tailor's shop, across the road," said Mel. "I recognize one of them from the other day with those two yobs at mums flat."

"Are you sure they're the same ones? They all look alike to me doll," said Cindy.

While Cindy was concerning herself about the escorts, Mel had counted out the money, and the shopkeeper was recounting it.

"Exactly right, Madam I'll throw in a couple of pairs of gloves for free," he said. He placed the little card carefully in a small box and wrapped it carefully. "Treat it careful, won't you. It's been around a long time and will damage easily."

"I will," Mel promised, heading for the door with her purchase safely tucked away in her handbag.

Outside the shop she asked, "Where to now, Cindy? That's my bit done," said Mel.

"We would like you to come with us, ladies, if you don't mind," said the nasal voice of Majeed from behind them. Cindy was about to turn around when she felt the sharp prick of the fine bladed knife through her coat.

"I, I… thought you were here to look after us," protested Cindy.

"We are. But we have some questions to ask you about your friends, Jaleel and Beg," sneered Majeed. A black BMW with dark tinted windows pulled up next to the curb and they were bundled in the back unceremoniously. The driver was another Arab and he was careful to pull away slowly into the traffic.

"Hamdulla!! They have been snatched from under our very noses."

"Taxi!!!" Asif shouted, stepping out into the road and making a passing cab brake hard to avoid him.

"Watch it," shouted the cabby through the open window. Asif was in the cab before he completed the words. He was quickly followed by Omar.

"Follow that car and if you don't lose it, I will reward you well," ordered Asif.

"Been waiting for someone to say that all me life, guv," replied the driver pulling out into the traffic. "What's on then?" asked the driver.

"Oh, just saw my girlfriend get in that car with another man, and I want to know what is going on," lied Omar.

Kaleel drove to the old docklands and into an abandoned warehouse.

When Masood finds out you have done this, he will have you fired," protested Cindy.

"I do not think so," replied Majeed, smiling and running his hand up Mel's leg, and she was terrified.

"Get your hands off her, you dirty bastard," shouted Cindy. Smack! The slap across her face sounded like a pistol shot. She recoiled into the seat.

"Any more of that, and I'll cut you up, just for the fun of it, slut. In my country, women do what they are told and do not speak badly to a man," warned Majeed.

"Fuck your country," spat Cindy.

Smack! This time a tooth flew out and she spat blood.

"Make you feel big slapping a woman around does it?" she challenged.

They were bundled out of the car and onto two chairs in the corner of the warehouse.

"What are you going to do with us?" whimpered Mel through floods of tears.

"A little information is all we want, and then you can go. But not until you have given us some of the pleasure you have given that little excuse for a man, Beg," sneered Majeed. Mel's flesh was crawling as he said it.

"I would rather die than give you any pleasure you pig," she spat.

"That can be arranged if you want it that way, my dear, but I will have my way first, be sure of that," said Majeed. With his knife digging into her ribs, his other hand slid up her skirt making her squirm. She gagged back the scream, afraid he would stab her there and then. Cindy looked on in disgust and horror. They had, by now, each been securely tied to a chair and there was nothing she could do to help her friend.

"Leave her alone you animal," ordered Cindy.

"Mind your own business bitch, or you will be next," threatened Majeed. Kaleel was eying Cindy up and down and it made her flesh crawl. She had met some creeps in her time at the club, but he was the worst of all.

CHAPTER NINETEEN
Only an Hour of Darkness

For Masood and Ali it was a quick change over from the private jet to the flight to Stockholm. The hotel had already arranged for suitcases to be placed on the flight, so it was a simple matter of a car taking them from one plane to another.

"I am glad to be out of that plane, Masood. I thought that stewardess, Helga, was going to eat me alive."

"Yes. She did rather look like a crocodile eying up a tasty meal and you were to be the meal," Masood laughed.

The flight lasted around three hours, but they slept most of the way in the comfy first class seats, undisturbed by cabin staff, who knew instinctively when a passenger wanted attention, or not. Only once during the flight did Masood get up, and that was to go to the curtain and check to see if their escort had made this flight. They were there, and from this Masood surmised they must have bribed a member of the hotel staff, who had tipped them off about the luggage. It was a point to remember for the future.

On arrival, they checked into the hotel and after a shower, went out to explore the city and have dinner.

"I do not understand, Masood. It is past ten in the evening and it is still like midday."

"Yes Ali, it's something to do with being nearer the North Pole. In the winter, it is dark nearly all the time, and in the summer light nearly all the time."

"Oh I couldn't cope with that," decided Ali.

"Good job, we're only here for a few days then isn't it?" said Masood.

"It is daylight and yet a lot of the cars drive around with their headlights on all the time. Are they mad here?" asked Ali.

After dinner, they caught a taxi back to the hotel and Ali could not help noticing that the driver's seat was encased at the back in very thick Perspex, as if to protect the driver. "Why is your seat so strange?" asked Ali.

"How do you mean strange, Sir?"

"Well, it's covered in thick Perspex. Is that in case of an accident and if so, is that because you're a bad driver?" continued Ali.

The driver laughed. "No Sir. I am a good driver. The Perspex is for my protection from passengers who want to attack me for my takings, or who don't want to pay the fare."

"Is it that bad here? We don't even get that where I come from in Bombay," said Ali.

"Yes. It can be bad and a few drivers have been killed Sir, so the police make us have these special seats fitted for our own protection." He dropped them off at the hotel and Ali paid him, and thanked him for the interesting journey.

"God Masood! I wouldn't want to live here would you?" asked Ali.

"No thanks. I am glad we will be gone in a few days.

"It's too cold here for me anyway, even in summer," confirmed Masood.

They went straight to bed and were up early the following morning to go out sightseeing. Many of the buildings are very old in Stockholm and the architecture fascinated Masood. At lunchtime, they found a restaurant which offered a buffet lunch, known as a smorgasbord.

"This meat is delicious and very lean. I wonder what it is," commented Ali. "Excuse me," he said stopping a passing waiter. "What is this meat?"

"Sir, It is reindeer. Tastier than beef and locally bred," answered the waiter.

"Thank you. Never would have thought of that," replied Ali continuing his meal.

They left the restaurant and returned to the hotel for a nap, as they were planning on seeing a bit of the nightlife later.

It was seven in the evening when they woke up and Ali was confused. "Is that reception?" he asked.

"Yes Sir," said the voice.

"What time is it?" he asked.

"Seven fifteen, Sir," said the bemused voice.

"Yes I know that," snapped Ali. "But is it morning or evening?"

"Ah! Evening Sir," said the voice with a knowing tone. "This is a common question, Sir. People get confused a lot."

"Thank you," said Ali hanging up the phone.

They showered and changed into casual clothes for the evening. Ali wore a light blue silk shirt, and white trousers and black shoes. Masood chose black trousers, a black shirt, a white tie, and a dark blue jacket.

They left the hotel and headed for a nearby restaurant which the receptionist had recommended.

"Did you see that man?" asked Ali.

"What man?" replied Masood.

"The one who just went past us," said Ali, pointing at the man heading down the street.

"No why?"

"He just came out of that shop with the blanked out windows and he had something tucked into his coat," said Ali.

"So?"

"So it must be a porn shop. Shall we have a look, we might be able to buy some sex toys for the girls," laughed Ali.

"Don't you ever think of anything else?" asked Masood.

They entered the shop and were amazed to see it was not a sex shop, but the shelves were stacked with bottles of spirits, of every kind you could imagine.

"May I help you gentlemen?" asked the man behind the counter, smiling at them.

"I, I'm not sure" said an embarrassed Ali. "I thought this was a sex shop with your windows all blanked out and everything."

"No Sir. We sell what you see. No sex things in here, but there is a shop up the road which has a good selection, I believe," replied the shopkeeper, smiling.

"Sorry," apologized Ali. So why are your windows blanked out?"

"Ah well, you see Sir, in Sweden we believe in free love. Sex shops are ok, but alcohol is not so good. It is tolerated, but many people don't like it and my customers are ashamed, so they hide their purchase in their coat as soon as they leave here. Just like the English hide their sex trade away."

"Now I understand," replied Ali. "Thank you for your time."

They left without buying anything which did not surprise the shopkeeper at all. Further up the street, they found the sex shop they had been told about, with many interesting things on open display in the window.

"Are you going in Ali?" asked Masood.

"Yes," was Ali's reply as he opened the door. It was like an Aladdin's cave for sex objects, toys and magazines. Masood, to his surprise, found something of interest straight away.

"Sir has discerning taste," said the voice of the blonde bombshell behind him. He turned to see who was addressing him to find a statuesque blonde of gorgeous proportions staring down at him from her six foot four position.

Dressed from head to foot in leather, her jacket half zipped as her large breasts tried to force the rest of the jacket open. She must have been about a size eighteen, but it was all in proportion and in the right places. Her blonde hair framed her smiling face.

"It is a speciality of the shop, Sir. You will not find one for sale anywhere else in the world." She was speaking about the leather whip he was holding, or rather caressing.

"Yes I like it. But it is made of more than leather, is it not?" Masood asked.

"Yes. It is leather, but then it is coated with special glue, and then dipped in fine sand. That gives it the coarse touch, and when used, unlike any other whip, instead of just leaving a mark, this one actually ever so lightly tears the skin," explained the blonde.

"Sounds fantastic," said Masood hoarsely.

"It is, Sir. It is. Would you like a demonstration, we have a room at the back."

Her invitation was spoken in a way that left no doubt she would love to flail the skin from Masood's back and, truth be told, he was briefly tempted.

"Thank you for the offer, but I must decline. I will, however, take two of the whips."

"That will be four hundred English pounds Sir," she said, disappointment clearly showing in her voice. Ali, meanwhile, could find nothing which could match his own offering, so he left disappointed. The smile on Masood's face told a different story.

They abandoned trying to find the restaurant, or any nightlife, but went back to the hotel and ordered food in their suite. They ate their meal in silence, each lost in his thoughts about Mel or Cindy, little knowing what drama was taking place in London. The next morning, the expected envelope arrived and Masood made the required call. By noon, they were on the plane back to Monte Carlo.

CHAPTER TWENTY
Unseen Danger

On arrival back in Monte Carlo, there was a message waiting for them from Greenberg saying that initial alterations had been made to the 707. He would like them to contact him and arrange to go to Hamburg to view and approve the aircraft, before further permanent modifications took place.

"Are you not excited?" asked Ali.

"Yes. I will call Greenberg in the morning and arrange to go to Hamburg as soon as we can. The girls will be back in a few days and I don't want them to know anything about this until it is ready for our test flight," said Masood smiling.

"Oh that is an excellent idea. They will be really surprised." Ali was so excited. Anyone would have thought he was buying the plane instead of Masood.

Masood spent the evening thinking of the new toy he had bought, and how he would enjoy Cindy using it on him. The thought sent tingles of pleasure down his spine.

"Good morning Mr Greenberg. I got your message. When would you like us to fly out?" asked Masood.

"Good morning. I will send an aircraft for you at any time you wish. Shall we say tomorrow morning around ten at the airport?"

"Sound's fine to me Greenberg. See you at ten then."

"Tell him not to have that Helga on board," pleaded Ali, pacing around the room getting very agitated.

But it was too late. Greenberg had already rung off.

"Call him back, please Masood," pleaded Ali.

"Don't be so silly. You can handle her if you want to. She's only a stewardess for God's sake," laughed Masood.

"I have a bad feeling about her Masood. A really bad feeling," said Ali wringing his hands.

"Correct me if I'm wrong Ali, but have you ever been right about one of your so called bad feelings?"

"No Masood, but there is always a first time."

"Then shut up about it and let's go eat."

It was pure coincidence that as Masood and Ali were flying to Hamburg to see the alterations, the Libyans had snatched Mel and Cindy, but Saeed hated coincidences.

Meanwhile, Asif and Omar back in London, had managed, with the help of their keen taxi driver, to follow Kaleel, Majeed and the girls to the warehouse.

"Want some help guv?" asked the taxi driver. "I know some big lads who will kick the shit out of them guys for you for a bob or two. Your girl will never know it was you," offered the taxi driver.

"No thanks. We can deal with it from here," said Asif, as he gave the driver all the money he had.

"You sure guv? There's about five hundred quid here."

"Yes! Yes! Just take it and go. If you come to the Waldorf tomorrow, there will be an envelope for you. What's your name," asked Asif.

"Sid Sir."

"Ok. Bye Sid."

Omar had already reached the warehouse and was looking through a dirty window, trying to make out what was happening inside. All the years of grime on the windows made it hard to see anything at all.

The slapping noises told them all they needed to know. They did not have time to ask for orders, but had to do what they thought was best, and risk the consequences later.

Staying together, they quickly circled the building looking for a different entrance to the one used by Kaleel and Majeed.

"This door is open," whispered Asif, gently opening the door and praying it would not creak.

They could hear voices as they crept into the dim interior of the warehouse. It was daylight outside, but the filth of many years on the windows of the warehouse prevented much of the light from entering. They had to pick their way across the floor, which was littered with rubbish and boxes, bits of wood and broken glass from the skylights above. Only the light through the broken skylights made it possible to see anything at all. It took time, and it was time the girls did not have, as Kaleel warmed to his work.

Kaleel was going to enjoy his work and the scar on his face made him look even more sinister in the shadowy light of the warehouse.

"Now bitch," Kaleel spat at Cindy, "where does Masood get his information from?"

"I, I don't know what you're talking about. What information?"

"Don't get smart with me or I will let Majeed play with your friend some more. He will enjoy that, but she won't," said Kaleel.

Mel was terrified and screwed her eyes up, not daring to look at either of the men. Then, she felt Majeed touch her hair and she screamed.

"No good doing that. No one to hear you around here," smiled Kaleel.

"Let me have a go at her," said Majeed.

"No, I have been looking forward to this for weeks and no one is going to rob me of my pleasure," snapped Kaleel. "Now where was I?"

"Talking to yourself?" spat Cindy. She didn't know what this was about and if she ever got out of this, Masood had some explaining to do. She wasn't going to make this easy for these bastards.

Cindy had been brought up on a tough housing estate in the East end of London, where threats were common-place and looking after yourself was second nature.

"Ah, yes. You were about to tell me where Masood gets his information from," said Kaleel.

"Let's kill them now," whispered Asif to Omar.

"No. We will listen for a while and see if they are successful or not. If not, then we can kill them both," whispered Omar.

"Sounds good to me," said Asif, running his fingers up and down the blade of a large throwing knife. They waited in the shadows, listening to Mel scream as Majeed ran his sweaty hands over her convulsing body. She vomited when Majeed ripped her bra off, but he did not care. He was enjoying this too much.

"Let me out of this chair, you bastard, and face me like a man. Let's see if you're as brave then," spat Cindy.

"Fancy your chances do you, little girl? You may be able to handle the drunks in the whore houses you work in but not a real man," said Kaleel sneering.

"I would like to see you take on my man," challenged Mel, taking them all by surprise and biting Majeed.

"Ow! You bitch." cried Majeed grasping his hand.

Smack! The slap was hard and made her head spin for a moment, but at least she felt better for having bitten him. Cindy started to scream.

"I told you it's no good doing that. No one will come," said Kaleel. He slapped her to stop her screaming. The high-speed buzz interrupted his words and instinctively, he dived to his left.

Asif's knife went over Kaleel's diving shoulder, and embedded itself in the throat of a shocked Majeed, who had chosen the wrong moment to stand up from playing with Mel's breasts, and unzipping his trouser fly. Instinctively, his hands went to his throat. Blood was gushing everywhere and splattering into Mel's hair. Unable to see what had happened, Mel instinctively screamed as the dying Majeed fell backwards, away from her. In his dying convulsion, Majeed grabbed her long hair on the way to the floor. Her chair, with her still tied to it, landed on his legs and the final nervous convulsions of his legs made it look as if he was trying to kick her off him. But for the tragedy, it would have been a comical sight.

She struggled and rolled the chair off his prone body, ending up lying next to him staring at his skewered neck. His blood was now staining the dust and concrete of the warehouse floor.

Kaleel ended his dive on the floor, and a bounding Omar was on him in a flash, but he threw the lighter Omar off.

"What is this, my brothers?" Kaleel demanded. "Do we not all want the same thing? Are we not all Arabs?"

"Don't call yourself my brother, you pig," retorted Omar.

"Nor mine," said Asif. "You torturer of helpless women, let's see how good you are against a man," challenged Asif.

"But there are two of you and I am alone, it is hardly fair," complained Kaleel.

"Who mentioned fair, you slimy bastard," spat Omar.

"So you both wish to die. So be it," replied Kaleel.

"Wait," shouted Cindy. "If anyone is going to kill this pig it should be me."

"You're either very brave or very stupid, slut," challenged Kaleel.

"I am neither. But I challenged you when I was tied up and my challenge stands. What have you to lose except your miserable life…?" Cindy sneered. "Or are you the coward I said you were?"

"I do not fight women," Kaleel snarled.

"No, you beat them up while they can't defend themselves. Is this your way of showing how strong you are? I spit on you," said Cindy.

Spttt!

"Cindy, don't be a fool. It is not worth dying for. You have Masood to think of," pleaded Mel as Asif cut her free.

"Masood!! He's the bastard that got me into this mess. When I see him again, I'll cut his balls off," shouted Cindy.

Asif and Omar were intrigued by this woman.

"If you wish you can fight him, but we will not interfere until one of you is dead," said Asif.

"That's fucking good enough for me," Cindy challenged.

"And if I win, what then?" Kaleel challenged.

"You fight one of us and if you win then you can go free," answered Asif.

"Done!!" agreed a smiling Kaleel. A knife appeared in his hand from nowhere.

Omar pulled his knife from Majeed's throat, and gave the knife to Cindy. Kaleel and Cindy, circled for a minute or two, each looking for an opening. The other three were watching, strangely fascinated. Kaleel lunged at Cindy, only missing her by a fraction, but she was quick and slashed his face as he overbalanced briefly. He wiped the blood from his face with the back of his hand, clearly surprised by her speed.

"Not as good as you thought are you bastard," she goaded.

"Good enough to skin you alive bitch," he retorted.

They continued to circle, until Cindy stumbled on something on the warehouse floor and Mel gasped. Cindy started to rise, but Kaleel was astride her, towering over her, grinning, his eyes ablaze and his arm rose about to deliver the killing blow.

Her knife came up from the ground with all her strength driving up through his exposed groin. Arrrrrrrggggrgggggg! His scream of pain and anguish must have been heard across London, as she twisted the knife through his bowels. Blood gushed all over her, but her hate was not finished yet. He crumpled, already dying as she dodged from under his buckling knees. Agony and surprise was etched deep into his contorted face and as he landed on his knees before toppling backwards. She lunged and buried the blood-soaked blade deep into his chest with all the hate she could muster. His dead eyes stared back at her from the warehouse floor. She was screaming at him now and beating his face with her fists. The years of hate for what her father and Bill had tried to do to her, all those years ago, and the beatings her mother had taken, releasing from her in violent passion.

Mel, Asif, and Omar stood dumbstruck as she rose from the floor covered in blood.

Omar was the first to speak, as he held her by her blood-soaked shoulders. "Hamdulla…Magnificent!! I have never seen such a thing. I thought when you stumbled you were dead."

His words went unheard by Cindy, as the shock set in. A tearful Mel took her friend in her arms and guided her to one of the chairs they had been tied to.

Omar went off to find a phone. Within half an hour, they were in an embassy car on the way to a bath and clean clothes. Cindy did not speak as the embassy staff stripped and bathed her, nor when they dressed her and put her in a car to The Waldorf.

Mel managed to get Cindy to the room before the floodgates opened. It was a toss up who cried most. In the small hours, sleep came and with it peace, at least for now.

CHAPTER TWENTY ONE
Flight into Danger

It was a lovely day when they took off for Hamburg to see the 707.

"Good morning, Greenberg. I did not expect you to come for us personally," said Masood.

"Good morning. It is the least I can do for a valued client, such as yourself Masood."

They were soon seated and the aircraft took off.

"Good morning, Sir. May I get you a drink?" Ali's heart missed a couple of beats, and sank, as he realized the dreaded Helga was on duty.

"Thank you Helga. I will have whisky," replied Ali.

"You have remembered my name, Sir. I am flattered," said Helga.

"How could I forget you?" replied Ali, embarrassed. They had been in the air about half an hour when the pilot's voice interrupted their conversation.

"I am sorry to announce that we have a problem with one of the engines and I have to divert to another airfield," came the voice over the public address system.

"Are we going to crash?" Ali asked Helga.

"No Sir. I am sure the pilot can handle it and there is probably only a small problem," Helga reassured. "The pilot is just being careful." They landed at a small club airfield and taxied to a halt.

"Where are we Helga?" asked Greenberg.

"At the end of the road, as far as you're concerned, you slimy bastard," she replied, turning and shooting him in the head. The shot splattered the cream-coloured interior of the plane with the bloody and grey mess of Greenberg's brains.

"What the hell…" was all Masood got out before Helga pushed the gun barrel up against his left temple?

"You ask too many questions. But the answer is, you are our prisoners and we will hold you for ransom," sneered Helga.

A single shot came from the cockpit area of the plane made them all jump.

"Karl just took early retirement on health grounds Helga," said the pilot's voice over the intercom.

"You can't. You don't know what you are doing," protested Ali.

"Shut up or I will blow your cock off, and that would be a great shame, for I have use for it in the coming days," Helga laughed.

"But," Ali started to say.

Click went the revolver as she cocked it and pushed it down into his groin.

"I will not warn you again," she threatened, leaving no doubt that she meant it.

A car had pulled up outside. The steps were lowered and they were bundled out of the plane and hoods fitted over their heads.

"Get in the car," growled a new voice. "Do anything we don't like and we will blow something off!!! Do we make ourselves clear?"

They nodded their agreement. Ali was not the soft touch Helga had mistaken him for, and he was already planning to cut her heart out slowly, if and when, he got the chance. They travelled for several hours and it was impossible to guess how far they had gone.

It would be a while before Greenberg and the plane were missed, and their captors intended to be a long way away by then. It was late afternoon by the time they arrived at the large old house deep in the forest. They had been driving for ages, but Masood was not sure they had gone a long way, or just a long way around.

"Get out," Helga ordered. "And don't try to escape or we will shoot one of you."

"We're of no value to you dead," retorted Masood.

"You're of no value to us at all at the moment, so don't get stupid," replied Helga.

By this time, Saeed had already flown over the airfield where the plane and Greenberg's body were.

"At least this time, we know where they are going," said Saeed confidently.

If only they had known that at the exact same time this conversation was taking place, they were passing over the airfield where the plane and the now dead Greenberg were lying undiscovered. They arrived at the airfield in Hamburg at about the same time as Masood and Ali were entering the house in the forest.

On arrival at Hamburg, Saeed could find no sign of the aircraft Masood had travelled on. It took a few phone calls and some diplomatic string-pulling for him to find out that they had no record of the plane having landed.

"I will call Greenberg's office and see what the hell is going on. We must not lose Masood again. There will be no forgiveness this time," said a worried Saeed. It took some time to find Greenberg's number, but he eventually got through.

"Good afternoon. My name is Saeed, and I am a friend of Mr Masood Jaleel. I need to speak to him as a matter of great urgency. I understand he was flying to Hamburg with your Mr Greenberg today. May I please speak to him or Mr Greenberg?"

"Just one moment Sir," said the voice at the other end of the line.

"Good afternoon Sir. I am Mr Greenberg's PA, how can I help?"

"I have a friend, Masood Jaleel, who was visiting your hanger workshop today and I am trying to contact him. It is a matter of some urgency."

"Yes Sir, I understand, but I cannot help you. Your friend left Monte Carlo with Mr Greenberg on one of our jets this morning, and we have not heard from them since. In fact, we have lost radio contact with the pilot, and have now contacted the police and air traffic control along their route, but there have been no reports of any aircraft coming down. So at the moment, it could just be a technical problem with their radio, and they may have returned to Monte Carlo," said the PA.

"No, my dear. They are not in Monte Carlo. I have checked Mr Jaleel's hotel in Monte Carlo and they have not returned."

"Please give me your number Sir, and if I get any news I will contact you. That is all I can do for now." He gave her the number and rang off.

"I knew it. I had a feeling our surveillance was going too well and now we have lost them. The shit will hit the fan now when Tehran find out," raged Saeed to no one in particular.

He was right. When Abdul Aziz got the news, he went mad.

"How the hell have you managed to lose them again? You will be replaced," he ranted into the phone.

"But, it was not my fault," pleaded Saeed hearing the border post calling.

"Do not interrupt me. What do you need to find them? We will use all diplomatic channels necessary," Abdul Aziz continued.

"No! Please don't do that. We are sure we can find them. It may just be a technical problem with the radio and they have had to land somewhere unexpectedly. Let us have at least twenty-four hours before we press the panic alarm," pleaded Saeed.

"Ok. But after that, your career is ended and you will be replaced. You know what that means?"

"Yes," was Saeed's reply. The posting to a dusty border post between Iran and Iraq for the rest of his life was calling his name.

It was a restless night for everyone, not least Ali, who was receiving the unwanted attentions of Helga. The house they had been taken to was an old hunting lodge which was in a state of disrepair.

"Why have you kidnapped us? We are not worth anything," pleaded Ali.

"That would be why you own one of the top hotels in Monte Carlo and were looking at buying a plane," growled a new addition to the group.

"Who are you?" asked Masood.

"That's my business. But I can assure you, it will not be a pleasure to meet me. As for why we have taken you, it's simple, you have money we want some of it. The more we get and the sooner, the less it will hurt. Am I making myself clear?"

"As crystal," chirped up Masood, getting a smack in the mouth for his attitude.

"There is no point in pretending to be brave. We are miles from anywhere in a house which people have forgotten exists. It is well guarded and there is only one approach road. If we are attacked, you will be dead before they can rescue you, and we don't mind if we die for our cause," sneered the new addition to the group.

"Seem to have it all covered don't you?" replied Masood. "So, when and where do you send the ransom note smart-arse?"

Crack.

He got another smack for that. He raised his hand to his split lip to wipe away the blood.

"That is up to you to tell us, my friend, and the sooner you do that, the less painful it will be."

"How much are you going to ask for?" Ali asked.

"Ten million Deutsche marks," was the reply.

"I haven't got my cheque book with me or I would write it out now and we could all go home," answered Masood.

"I don't like you, Masood. You're a smart bastard and I hate smart bastards."

"I was only trying to help. After all, none of my staff have any authority to draw out that kind of money and I don't have any family either. You should have done your research better before you grabbed us. We're no use to you at all," laughed Masood.

The group left the room, leaving Ali and Masood locked in and helpless.

"So what the hell do we do with them now? He is right. We have no way of getting a ransom for them," said an angry Helga.

"Shut up, Helga. Let me think."

"You think. I'm going back to have some fun with Ali," replied Helga defiantly.

"No, you're not. Leave him alone. Don't you ever think of anything else?"

"Yes, but he is so well equipped it would be a pity to waste it when I kill him. I want to get as much fun out of it as I can before I shoot him."

"You stupid sex-mad bitch, you could kill him and then there would be no ransom."

"We have to work out a way of getting the ransom from them. The problem is, they have no one else to get the money for them," said the new voice. The new voice belonged to Herman, the leader of the group, a hard evil-looking man with a crooked smile.

That remark even got Helga's mind off Ali for a while.

"What if we take one of them to the bank and keep the other one here. The one we take won't try anything because his friend will get it if he does," suggested Herman.

CHAPTER TWENTY TWO
Needle in a Haystack

"What do you think they will do with us, Masood? Will they kill us anyway, even when we get them the money?" asked Ali.

"No. You worry too much. They won't harm us, and anyway our friends will probably turn up in the nick of time and kill them all. Then we will go back to Cindy and Mel," said Masood, without too much conviction. He did not want to worry Ali who, if he decided they were going to die anyway, was likely to try to take as many of these rats with him as he could, and Masood was just getting used to the good life. He was not ready for dying just yet.

The room they were in was dark and stank of stale pee. Its only furniture was two tatty old armchairs, with lots of torn fabric, and they smelled worse than the room.

"There is lots of hope. My shoes are bugged," assured Masood.

"What do you mean?" blurted Ali.

"Shssh," Masood said, and indicated the same with his finger on his lips. Saeed, and the men who are following us, must have got very upset when we went to Monte Carlo by private jet and they lost us for a while."

"Yes," interrupted Ali.

"I was putting my shoes on the other day when I noticed a mark on the heel. As you know they are new, so I looked closer and I am sure the rubber heel had been removed. I checked my others and they had all been tampered with, so I guess we can expect the cavalry anytime now," assured Masood.

"Thank God for that! I never thought I would say this, but I will be glad to see them," said Ali.

The fuel-tanker driver pulled on to the local landing field, as he did every two weeks, to fill up the tanks for the light aircraft, which flew from the field. It was not until he had filled up the tanks and was driving around the rear of the control tower building, that he saw the Lear jet parked at a strange angle with the door open.

There was no sign of anyone around which was strange, so he stopped his truck and went to investigate. It was the smell that hit him first as he mounted the aircraft steps, then the squeaks from the rats scurrying around what was left of poor Greenberg's head.

Urrghhh! He threw up on the aircraft floor before rushing from the plane out into the fresh air, gasping for breath. He rushed over to the empty building and used his emergency key to open the office, and quickly rang the police.

The blare of the sirens as the police arrived was deafening, but he was relieved to have other people around.

An officer got out of the lead car as it screeched to a halt next to the aircraft.

"My name is Baum, Otto Baum. You found the body," he demanded of the still shaken driver.

"Ja," replied the driver.

"Good. Please go with my sergeant. He will take your statement."

Baum turned and ran up the steps of the aircraft, reeling slightly as he got to the top and was hit by the smell.

"We have found this note Sir," said a young policeman, using the up-held note to hide his face which was turning a pale shade of green. His vomit missed Baum by inches as the young policeman ran for the open door.

Baum read the note, and placed it carefully into a plastic bag, before carrying on inspecting the inside of the aircraft.

Soon the ambulance arrived, closely followed by the forensic team, who quickly started to go through the aircraft in a meticulous search for any clues.

Meanwhile, Baum contacted Greenberg's office and broke the bad news. It was an hour later that Heidi composed herself enough to call Saeed.

"Good morning, is that Mr Alman?"

"Yes who is this?"

"It's Heidi, Mr Greenberg's PA. I am afraid I have some bad news," she said, before her voice cracked and she was sobbing.

"What is it my dear?" Saeed urged, his heart sinking into his shoes. For God's sake, don't let them be dead he thought.

"I am afraid…" she sniffled on. "They have found our aircraft on a remote airfield and Mr Greenberg has been murdered." She broke down again before a man's voice came on the line.

"Please excuse Heidi, Mr Alman, but she has taken the news very badly. She had been with Mr Greenberg a long time, said Otto, Greenberg's project manager."

"Yes. Yes," Saeed snapped. "What of the others?"

"There are no signs of the others, but there is a note from the man who was the pilot, Hans. It tells us the others have been taken by a group from Bader Mienhoff, a vicious group of German terrorists. They are known as an evil lot and they are demanding a ransom of ten million Deutsche marks."

"Who is dealing with this matter?" demanded an irate Saeed. Otto gave him the details of the police station and the officer in charge.

"We are sorry this has happened," Otto apologized. Saeed had already hung up. Saeed was soon on his way out of the hotel and into a taxi. He gave the driver the details he had been given, and promised him a large tip to get him there as soon as possible. It was two hours before they reached their destination and the officer in charge was waiting for him.

"Good afternoon, Mr Alman. I am Otto Baum." Saeed shook the outstretched hand. It was cold, like its owner.

"I am afraid we have little to go on as yet. They were very thorough in clearing the plane, except for poor Mr Greenberg's brain which was left as a message, and the dead co-pilot."

"Do you know how important these two men are, Baum?"

"I do not like your tone, Alman?" said Baum.

"That's ok. You will get used to it in the end. Now, what are you doing to find these people?"

"As I told you, we have little to go on. They were taken away by car, but we have no idea where," explained Baum.

"It's a good job we're not reliant on you then isn't it?" replied Saeed sarcastically.

"Are you always this rude?" demanded Baum.

"When the safety of my country is at stake, yes I am," was Saeed's terse reply.

"I do not understand," said Baum.

"Luckily for me, you don't have to. Now, how many plain cars can you let me have with drivers who know the area? I will also need three radio-direction trucks," said Saeed.

"We don't have those. Only the Army has those."

"Then get them from the Army you clown or shall I go higher?" demanded Saeed.

By this time, Baum was bright red with fury.

"Get out of my office. I will not be spoken to in this manner," said Baum.

Saeed laughed mockingly.

"You really don't know what has happened, do you?" asked Saeed.

"No! What is so special? Anyway, I told you to get out."

"I will go, but before I do, may I use your telephone?" asked Saeed.

"No. You can use the phone in the reception area. Now for the last time, get out," demanded Baum who was clearly about to explode with fury.

Saeed left, and made a call from the phone in the reception area. His call to the Embassy was short and to the point and telephone lines started to buzz across the world. Twenty minutes later, he was back in Baum's office behind Baum's desk.

"If only you had explained," went on Otto Baum. "I have contacted the Army and the trucks are on their way as we speak."

CHAPTER TWENTY THREE
The Search Begins

"Fortunately, the men we are looking for will not know that Masood has trackers in the heels of his shoes. As long as we can get within a hundred miles of them, we can find them. We can then use the three trucks to pinpoint where they are and we can go and get them," confided Saeed.

"My men will be ready and at your disposal," replied Baum.

"Thank you, but I will not need them. I have the best men for the job, and you could say each of them has a vested interest in nothing going wrong," said Saeed, pacing up and down the drab office Baum had assigned to him. The desk had been covered in dust until a few hours before, but had been quickly cleaned. A telephone had been installed along with several office chairs for the group to use. It had been a store room which had been hurriedly cleared, but the grimy windows let little light in and of the three ceiling lights only one worked, but it served its purpose.

"If that is what you wish," replied Baum.

"It is the way it has to be. Now, when are we getting these damn trucks?" Saeed demanded impatiently.

It seemed like many hours before the trucks arrived, but was in fact less than an hour. Baum had used his local knowledge to work out a search pattern and they started as soon as the trucks arrived.

"I have just heard from our local contact that they have started a search for our visitors," reported Helga to Herman, the leader of the group.

"Let them look. They will never find us here, and if they try, it will be curtains for them. The woods are booby-trapped and we will be gone, if there are any survivors trying to find us," laughed Herman.

"You will of course kill us anyway, won't you?" challenged Masood.

"What makes you think that?" retorted Herman.

"Because you have made no attempt to hide your identities from us, so it is obvious you intend to leave no witnesses," replied Masood.

"You could be right, but you're not. You see, we don't care about you knowing who we are. We were all wanted anyway before we got you, with the exception of Hans and Helga, but they can hardly return to their jobs now can they? They will join the rest of us on the wanted list," said Herman. He smiled. It was not a pleasant smile, but that of a maniac enjoying his victim's fear.

"Now, perhaps you will understand why I said we are all prepared to die for our cause. If they attempt a rescue, you and your friend go first, said Herman. "For example I am wanted for many crimes but most of all for the bomb I planted in a Munich car factory which killed many foreign workers," he stated proudly.

It was a flawless argument and one Masood had given no thought to at all. For the first time, he felt fear and it was a strange sensation. How ironic, he thought, that he should go to all this trouble to become rich, and the only reason he and Ali were in this mess is because they're rich. The girls would be back in Monte Carlo soon and they would be worried when they found Ali and Masood were gone, and there would be no news of an official search. The reason he and Ali were so important, could hardly be announced on the evening news.

"You look worried, Masood. Have they said something while I was in the bathroom? It stinks in there," said Ali.

"Yes," agreed Masood.

"What did they say? Are they going to kill us?" Ali asked.

"No, Ali. I was agreeing it stinks. But then, the whole house stinks. I am not worried about us, just thinking of Cindy," Masood lied.

"I have been thinking of Mel a lot, and what I will tell her when we get out of this mess. I have decided I will tell her about what Helga did and take my chances. I don't want any secrets from her," said Ali.

"Not sure that's a good idea. After all, it was not your fault what Helga did. Why upset Mel about it?" asked Masood. "You don't have to tell her because of me. I promise I won't tell if you don't," assured Masood.

They had not heard Helga come into the room, as the door was covered with an old Army blanket to reduce the draughts.

"I have lots of plans for you, Ali and they don't include your girlfriend," said Helga smiling.

"I don't care what your plans are, I won't be doing anything with you, you bitch," spat Ali defiantly.

"Temper, temper Ali, I want us both to enjoy what is to come, if you'll excuse the pun," laughed Helga.

"Don't upset him Helga. He will cut your black heart out if he gets the chance," warned Masood.

"This is useless," growled Saeed. "We have been searching all day, and not a bleep on any of the trucks. They could be hundreds of miles away and we may never find them."

"How will they get the money from this Masood?" asked Baum.

"How the hell do I know," snapped Saeed.

"Has he got any relatives they can contact, or could his staff pay it?" asked Baum.

"I doubt the staff could get at that amount of money and, as far as I am aware, he has no relatives. If he does, they will be in India," replied Saeed.

"Then we must continue to look and hope for a break, or for them to make a mistake, said Baum." Also, I have contacted all banks and they will contact us if anyone requests the amount of the ransom," continued Baum.

CHAPTER TWENTY FOUR
Payment on Demand

"Helga. You and Hans are to take Masood into Hamburg to the bank," ordered Herman.

"Why me?" demanded Helga.

"I don't trust you to be left with the other one. And because I said so, or are you the leader now?" demanded Herman.

"No. When shall we go?" replied Helga lowering the tone in her voice. She hated Herman; he was ruthless and cruel and would not hesitate to kill anyone who questioned his leadership.

"Now is as good a time as any. Remember, don't let him talk to any of the bank staff alone," ordered Herman.

"I'm not stupid you know," replied Helga.

She entered the room Ali and Masood were in.

"Masood, you're coming with us. Ali, you are lucky as you're staying with my friends," smiled Helga, brushing her hand across his head.

"Where are we going?" asked Masood as they bundled him out of the house towards a waiting car.

"Just get in the car. You will know when we want you to know," growled Helga.

It took them two hours to drive into Hamburg. For most of the journey, Masood was laid down on the back seat.

"If you try to look where we're going one more time, I'll put a bag over your head," warned Hans.

"That would look good as we got out of the car," replied Masood, earning himself a punch in the ribs.

"Next time, I'll break some of them.Then we will see if you're still a smart-mouth," snapped Hans.

On arrival at the bank, they went in together, with Masood looking a little the-worse-for-the-journey. Being face down in the car most of the time had made him a little car sick, and he was pale and drawn, as they approached the counter

"Yes Sir. What can I do for you? Are you alright?" asked the cashier.

"Yes, thank you. I would like to see the manager if it is possible," replied Masood.

"I will see what I can do, Sir. What is your name?"

"Masood Jaleel and I have an account with your head office in Geneva."

The cashier was gone for a few minutes and returned with a small man accompanying her. He introduced himself as the manager.

"I am pleased to meet you, Mr Jaleel. If you would come to the office at the end of the counter, I would be happy to see if I can help you," said the manager.

He had already checked who Masood was and was keen to grovel. He wore a dark grey suit with a fine pinstripe. He was about fifty years old and wore small round spectacles, which perched on his nose making him look like an owl.

"Please take a seat and tell me how we can help," invited the manager.

"I need to make a large withdrawal," said Masood.

"How large is large, Sir?" the manager asked.

"Ten million Deutsche marks," replied Masood.

"That is a large amount of money. Sir, may I ask the purpose?"

Helga was just about to tell him he could not, when Hans crushed her foot.

"Ouch!" gasped Helga.

"Sorry," apologized Hans, taking the chance to whisper a caution in her ear. It did not go unnoticed by the keen eyed manager.

"I regret, Sir, that we do not keep such a large amount in the bank. We can certainly arrange a draft if that is alright?" offered the manager, keen to please.

"No. It has to be cash. When could you get it for me?" asked Masood.

"We could certainly get it here for the day after tomorrow," promised the manager, remembering the telex message he had received from his German head office that morning. "You understand we have to arrange security for that amount."

"That would be fine," answered Masood.

"Good. Then I will make the arrangements and it will be ready for collection on Thursday," confirmed the manager. "Is there anything else I can do for you today?" he grovelled.

"No thank you," said Masood, rising from his seat and heading for the door. The manager was at the door and opening it in a flash, shaking Masood's hand as he left.

"That was easy," stated Helga, as they left the bank heading for the car. "And you were bright not to try anything because if we are not back in five hours, your friend dies."

"You like saying that, don't you bitch," said Masood. "There will come a day when I may stuff those words down your pretty throat, just before Ali slits it for you."

They were in the car when she stuck the gun in his face.

"Listen you pig, if anyone is going to get killed it will be you and it will be me doing the killing," Helga snapped. She pistol whipped him across the head before Hans could stop her.

"For God's sake we need him in good condition to get the cash you stupid bitch," Hans barked.

The rest of the drive back was done in silence.

"How did it go?" asked Herman, when they arrived back at the old house.

"It went well. They will have the cash ready on Thursday," answered Hans with a smile.

"Good, good, and did he behave himself?" asked Herman.

"Yes. He was good," said Hans.

"Then, why is his head bleeding?" demanded Herman.

"Oh, because Helga couldn't resist hitting me?" sneered Masood.

Smack!

The sound caught everyone by surprise.

"I will not tell you again Helga," Herman shouted, as she reeled across the room. "If you touch either of them again, without my order, I will kill you. We need them, or are you too stupid to understand that?"

"N, no," Helga muttered, picking herself up off the floor. I'm going to shoot this arrogant bastard when this is over, she decided as she left the room and went upstairs.

"We have a break at last," announced Baum, as he came into his office.

"What is it?" demanded Saeed.

"I placed an alert to the banks for them to report if anyone tried to draw out the amount of the ransom. A branch of a Swiss-based bank in Hamburg has just contacted us, to say that Masood Jaleel turned up today with a man and a woman, and he asked to withdraw ten million Deutsche marks in cash," said Baum beaming.

"Tell me they didn't give it to him," begged Saeed.

"No. The manager told them the bank didn't hold that amount in cash, but would have it ready by Thursday," explained Baum.

"Thank God for that. Now we have a chance to get them, and at least rescue Masood," smiled Saeed.

"Yes. I will call off the search, as we know where they will be on Thursday," said Baum.

"No don't do that. We have to keep looking, as they may have sympathizers who alert them. If we continue to look, who knows, we may find them before Thursday," cautioned Saeed.

"I am so looking forward to seeing Ali again," Mel confessed, as they sat on the plane on the way to Monte Carlo.

"Yes, Mel. I never thought I would say this about any man, but I have missed Masood a lot, and he has some serious questions to answer. Don't get me wrong, I enjoyed being back in London and seeing Mum and Johnny. I am so thrilled to have gotten Johnny into that private boarding school away from those bullies, but it would have been better with Masood along," said Cindy.

"Yes, I agree," said Mel, keeping the subject away from what had happened at the warehouse.

"Johnny is very excited about going to his new school. You should have seen their faces when I asked if there was a discount if I paid all the fees up until he was eighteen in advance," laughed Cindy.

"Did they knock anything off?" asked Mel.

"Ten percent. But it came to a tidy sum, so I invested it in a trust for Johnny until he is eighteen," said Cindy. "How did your Mum take the news about you marrying Ali?"

"Good, I suppose. Said she didn't mind what colour he was as long as he made me happy. If he didn't, she would cut his what's-it off," laughed Mel.

"Need a bloody big knife for that," laughed Cindy.

"I didn't tell her that bit. Thought she would think I was making it up," smiled Mel.

They passed the rest of the flight in idle chatter, unaware of the drama they were about to enter when they got back to the hotel.

"Mademoiselle Mel. Mademoiselle Cindy. It is so good to see you. I am so sorry about the news," greeted Bernard, the hotel manager.

"What news, Bernard?" asked Cindy.

"Why the news about Monsieur Masood and Monsieur Ali Mademoiselle," Bernard answered.

"We haven't heard any news. What the hell are you on about? Are they alright?" pleaded Mel.

"Mon Dieu, I do not know! They have been kidnapped by terrorists," confirmed a perplexed Bernard.

"Not funny Bernard. Not fucking funny," snarled Cindy. "Has that bastard Masood put you up to this? I will castrate the bastard when I find him."

"No Mademoiselle. No. This is not a joke, it is true. They went to Hamburg to buy a plane with a man called Greenberg, and he has been found dead in the plane they went in. There was a note saying Masood and Ali were kidnapped and they wanted a very big ransom," explained Bernard.

"I will pay it," cried Mel. "How much do they want?"

"I am sorry, but the police are not saying anything else. Bernard had led them into his office and sat them down and was busy pouring large brandies for them both. The police say it is safer if they keep as much as possible secret for now," said Bernard.

He was a tall man sickeningly thin and his face lined with many years of smiling at clients. He had brilliant white teeth and greying hair which made him look distinguished.

"I bet this has something to do with what happened to us in London. When I get my hands on Masood, he will wish he had never been born," said Cindy, gulping down the brandy.

They were halfway through the bottle of brandy before Mel stopped shaking.

"Bernard, get me the officer in charge on the phone. I want to talk to him and I mean now," barked Cindy.

"Oui, Mademoiselle," said Bernard, picking up the phone and dialling the number he had been given by Saeed. The officer on the other end promised to find Saeed and ring back.

The phone rang ten minutes later and though they had been waiting for it, they still jumped when it rang.

"Who is this?" demanded Cindy of the caller.

"I am Captain Saeed Alman. We met before, at the party in Masood's hotel when I rescued you from the slimy man from the casino and we had a dance."

"Yes. What are you calling for? I am waiting for an important call you idiot," chided Cindy.

"Yes, Mademoiselle. You asked Bernard to call me, and I am far from being an idiot," retorted Saeed sharply.

"Oh I'm sorry. I am so upset I don't know what to say," apologized Cindy, embarrassed.

"It is nothing, Cindy. May I call you Cindy?" asked Saeed.

"Yes. What is happening with Masood and Ali, and how come you're in charge of a case in Germany?" asked Cindy.

"First things first. I am in charge because that is the way it is, but you do not need to know any more than that. As for Masood and Ali, we are looking for them at present. We are confident we will find them soon," promised Saeed.

"What about the ransom? We will pay it," said Cindy getting frustrated.

"But you do not even know how much it is," said a surprised Saeed.

"Do you think we care? Mel and I have money and we will gladly pay any amount," said Cindy.

"Such is love," said Saeed.

"What?" Cindy demanded.

"I said, such is love," he repeated. "The amount is ten million Deutsche marks," said Saeed.

"How much is that in English money?" Cindy demanded.

"I don't know. As I have no intention of paying it, I don't care" said Saeed, abruptly.

"What do you mean you have no intention of paying it? I just said, we will pay it," said Cindy.

"It is not a question of who pays it. We know that Masood has already contacted his bank, and they will have the money ready on Thursday. Even if he pays the ransom, these people do not have a good record at handing hostages back," said Saeed.

"What is he saying Cindy? Tell me," begged Mel.

"He says it will be ok doll. They have the money, and are waiting for contact from the ransom gang. Then they will make an exchange," Cindy lied.

"So what do we do for now?" asked a distraught Mel wringing her hands.

"We wait doll, we wait," replied Cindy.

"But I hate waiting and the thought of my Ali in the hands of some kidnappers is just too much to bear. What if they hurt them, or don't let them go, even when they have the money?" challenged Mel.

"Steady Mel. It will be alright I promise," assured Cindy.

"How do you know that?" retorted the normally mild-mannered Mel, taking Cindy by surprise. "How the hell can you be so sure when the man I love is being held by maniacs?"

"Mel!!" shouted Cindy.

It was all Cindy got out before Mel rushed out of the office and up to the suite. Once inside, she threw herself on the bed sobbing.

Cindy followed her up to the suite. Once inside, she poured two large drinks and followed Mel into the bedroom gently closing the door behind her.

CHAPTER TWENTY FIVE
The Lair Is Found

"I have some more good news," said Baum down the phone to Saeed. "We have found them."

"That's great news," shouted Saeed.

"Yes. We found them during the night, but I did not bother you, as there was nothing we could do until daylight. They are in an old hunting lodge out in the forest," said Baum proud of the achievement.

"I want to be on the way there in an hour. Have three cars ready," Saeed shouted as he slammed the phone down. Hurrying down the hall he burst into the large room the group were using as a dormitory. It was a meeting room into which several beds had been placed for them to use in shifts.

"Get up you lot. We have work to do. The police have found them and now it's up to us to go in and get them out," urged Saeed.

Half an hour later, they met in Baum's office. He had a map spread across his desk when they arrived.

"This is where they are. It is about two hours away from here by road. I'll have two Army helicopters picking us up in ten minutes. We will be dropped about ten miles away so they won't hear us coming. The area is very dense forest and there is a single track leading to the road. A man and woman went to the house in a car this morning," said Baum.

"Good. Have they come out yet?" asked Saeed.

"No," Baum replied.

"Excellent! You say they came down the road to the right?" prompted Saeed.

"Yes," confirmed Baum, nodding his head.

"Then I want a heavy truck turned over on that road, just out of sight of the track turning around that bend," said Saeed jabbing his finger on the map.

"But where do I get a truck?" asked a confused Baum.

"Don't ask me. It's your country. Just do it and do it now. Don't use an Army truck," ordered Saeed.

Within an hour, the trap had been set. Another hour later, the man and woman came out of the hunting lodge and got in the car. They headed up the track and at the end, turned right. Just around the bend, they were met with the sight of the truck on its side blocking the road. Unsuspecting, they stopped and got hurriedly out to see if they could help the driver, who was hanging out of the shattered windscreen. His head and face covered in blood, but he seemed to be regaining consciousness.

"Are you alright?" asked the woman as she reached the injured driver.

"My legs are trapped. Please help me," the driver pleaded.

They bent down to look in the cab and see what they could do.

Phh, phh. They heard the noise as the driver shot them both with tranquilizer darts in the neck.

"Nicely done, Mayoub," smiled Saeed."Never knew what hit them. Now, let's get them out of here, while Baum's men clear up this mess."

The couple were taken back to Baum's police station where Yousef had been preparing two cells for them to be questioned in.

"Are you feeling better my dear?" she heard, as she started to come around from the tranquilizer.

"Who the…," she began to say.

Smack! Her lip split.

"No, no. I ask the questions, you provide the answers," said Saeed in a treacly voice.

She spat blood along with her defiant answer.

"If you're police, I have rights," she shouted.

"But we're not, and you don't, my dear," Saeed replied, in a voice which made her blood run cold. "All we want is some answers about your friends in the hunting lodge, and you can go."

"I will tell you nothing you pig," she spat defiantly.

"That's not nice. If you don't tell me, then I will set my friend Yousef on you. Believe me my dear, you will tell him," smiled Saeed.

One look at the smiling Yousef made her blood turn to ice. But she had always known this moment may come, and she was up to the test, or at least she thought she was.

CHAPTER TWENTY SIX
Terrorist Torture

Saeed played with her for an hour before he handed her over to Yousef. She was defiant, he would give her that. But in the hands of Yousef, she had no chance. Yousef had practised his art in the jails of Iraq and he was very good at what he did. The room they were in was furnished only with a bed with tall legs, a chair, and a coal fire. In a corner, was something scratching around, but it was too dark to see what it was. She hoped it was not a rat. She hated rats.

Yousef started by stripping her naked, then, with the help of Khalaf and Asif, she was lifted onto the tall bed which was covered in a plastic sheet. She struggled, but to no avail and two other men bound her to the bed with wide leather belts. The plastic was cold on her back at first, but her fear soon warmed that up. Yousef asked her some questions, but she was still defiant.

"You have spirit. I like that. It will make my job so much more interesting," Yousef sneered. "I am going to tell you what will happen to you," he gloated. "As you have seen, by the fire is a metal bucket. It is empty and has two large straps attached to it." He was savouring her growing fear now.

"I will place the bucket bottom up on your soft belly, but before I strap it down, my friend Asif is going to take the rat out of the cage in the corner and slip it under the upturned rim."

Her gasp at the mention of the rat did not go unnoticed by Yousef.

"The rat will be trapped in the bucket. Then the fun starts because I will place hot coals from the fire into the base of the bucket. Mr Rat is going to get hot and he can't eat through the bucket so he will eat through you, my dear. First your skin, then into your stomach," grinned Yousef, enjoying every minute of it. His bad breath in her nostrils added to her disgust.

She was retching and now terrified. She had not even noticed that, sat on the chair in the room, was the man who they had captured with her. Her eyes were rolling as Asif approached with the squirming rat in his gloved hand. It was brown with a very long tail and she remembered her childhood and the boy who had locked her in the woodshed on the mountainside until she gave him a kiss. There had been rats in that shed, and she had feared the dark and rats from that day on. The look on Yousef's face was of intense pleasure. Her fellow prisoner was busy being sick. Her eyes were bulging as Asif got closer. She gritted her teeth until they hurt and sweat poured from her. Her body glistened with sweat as Asif and the rat got nearer. They had chosen the one thing in the world she could not stand. She was petrified at the thought of it eating into her and, before it even touched her, she could feel the tiny teeth biting into her. Saeed sensed her panic rising and ordered her companion to be removed. But not before he saw Asif slide the rat into the upturned bucket and clamp it firmly down on her belly.

She was screaming now. She could feel the little feet running across her with its whiskers touching her skin, and its long tail dragging across her stomach as it moved. It was scampering around, not liking its prison, and any second would come the first bite. Sweat was pouring from every pore on her naked body as the rat continued its search for an escape route. Her nails were breaking as she dug them harder into the side of the bed. She was by now too terrified to feel the pain as they snapped.

"I, I will tell you anything. Just get it out," she screamed.

"Not just yet, my dear," said Saeed. Let us talk for a while and we will see if you have anything of interest before we deprive Mr Rat of his lunch."

"Wh!! what do you want to know?" she pleaded.

"I want to know who the people are at the house where you were this morning. How many there are. How they are armed and how the place is guarded. We will cross check what you tell us with your friend, and if it is true, we will keep you until after we have our friends back. Then you can go," said Saeed.

"How do I know I can trust you?" she asked.

"You don't, Saeed sneered. But then, I'm not the one with a trapped rat running around on my belly, am I?"

"There are five men and one woman in the house," she started. Our leader's name is Herman. Then there is Franz, Harold, Sven, Hans and Helga. The house is an old hunting lodge with seven bedrooms, a large living room, a dining room, and another room which has lots of old toys in it. Then there is a cellar off the main hall, and this is where your friends are kept. She went on talking faster, and faster, describing the inside of the house in great detail.

"Slow down my dear. We want it clearly," said Saeed.

But she was getting more worked up about the rat by the second.

"Asif take your friend away for a while. It may help her think more clearly. We don't want any mistakes, do we?" Saeed said sarcastically.

"Yes, Saeed," said Asif, loosening the straps and reaching under the bucket clearly disappointed.

She was relieved that he had removed the rat and started talking more calmly now. Although it did not matter that she had talked at speed before, because it was all being recorded for them to go over again later. He did not want her to get in such a state, that she forgot important details. Saeed was convinced she would tell him everything to avoid Asif's friend again.

"The woods surrounding the house are booby trapped with grenades and mines. You will not be able to get near the place without heavy casualties. As soon as they know they are being attacked, they will kill your friends," she continued.

"What are the patrols outside?" Saeed asked.

"There are always two guards outside and one roaming around inside, while the other three rest. Your friends are tied up in the cellar at the back. Everyone has a pistol and the outside guards have machine guns and grenades," she explained.

"Thank you my dear. You have been most helpful. Now, is there anything else you want to tell me before I talk with your friend?"

"No, nothing I promise. I have told you all there is to know," she pleaded, terror etched on her face.

"I believe you my dear," Saeed reassured her, patting her on the head. "I told you that you would tell Yousef everything and you have. Now you must excuse me. I have to have a chat with your friend. I hope he is as helpful as you have been."

"But what if he refuses to talk? Will you kill us both?" she pleaded.

"Kill! Kill! Who mentioned killing anyone? Do not worry, your friend will talk," Saeed smiled, as he said it and her blood turned to ice again as he left the room.

In another room, her friend was being prepared for his chat with Saeed. Yousef was hard at work and Khalaf was busy bringing in jug, after jug, of cold water. The man had been stripped and laid out on three domestic dining room chairs. He was face up with his head resting on one chair seat. His feet rested on another chair and the third had been placed under his bare buttocks. Yousef had bound his feet to the seat of one chair and his head was held to the other by a wide strap which fitted over his forehead and nose area. A clamp had been placed in his mouth to hold it open and hold his tongue in place so he could not swallow it. His hands were tied across his stomach.

There was a contraption dangling from the ceiling, above his groin area, which looked like two wooden rollers about an inch in diameter. The rollers were joined by a V-shaped piece of spring steel rod at each end, so that when you forced them apart anything inserted between the rollers would be squeezed by the rollers closing together. At the end of the spring steel, was a set of pulleys through which ran the steel cable to the hook in the ceiling. The effect of the contraption was that the rollers were placed over a victim's penis, and then allowed to close on the penis. The wire to the ceiling was tensioned just enough to hold the downward weight of the victim, when the chair supporting his buttocks was removed.

The victim was then in pain, but could do nothing. If he struggled, the pain increased. This was painful enough, but Yousef had added his personal touch, and this is where the water came in. The victim was then slowly forced to drink an ever increasing amount of water. Everyone knows how painful it can be when you can't find a toilet, but this is a hundred times worse, as you're not only bursting to relieve yourself, but your weight is growing, making the rollers squeeze harder. After his session with the woman, Yousef was warming to his task, and all the men had been betting on how long it would take before the man broke. With the strap over his eyes, the victim could not see what was about to happen, but his fear started to grow when the rollers were placed over his manhood and allowed to close. Yousef deliberately let them close slowly waiting for the man's gasp. He was not disappointed. They could just make out his curse, because of the face clamp.

"Now, my friend I have had a word with your lady friend and she has been most co-operative. But we need you to confirm some of her answers. You will use your fingers for this. If you want to confirm her answer you hold up one finger. If you don't agree, you hold up two. Do you understand one finger yes, two fingers no?" asked Yousef.

Another gurgled curse came out of the distorted mouth.

"Now…," said Yousef, "you are no doubt wondering what we are going to do, so I will explain. The contraption on your dick is pressure-operated and, at the moment, there is no pressure, as I have a chair under your arse. When I remove the chair..." The victim started to sweat. "…Like this…" Yousef pulled the chair out.

"Aaaaaagh!!!!" the scream lasted a long time.

"As you have found, there is pain you never knew possible. Don't sweat so much my friend, or we will have to put more water into you to replace that lost by you sweating," whispered Yousef.

Yousef took his time explaining to his victim, who was already in excruciating pain, what would happen.

"To start things off, my friend Khalaf will pour a jug of water into you. As you gain weight, so will the pain increase and your need for a pee will help your memory as well. At the end, if you can withstand all the pain, the contraption will end up ripping your balls out by the roots. I shall begin," announced Yousef.

He was a master at his art and though the man tried in vain to cough the water out, more went in than went on the floor. Saeed let him start screaming, before he asked the first question.

"Oh, I forgot to say, I am putting a few trick questions in. If you try to mislead me, I will let Khalaf put another gallon in you," promised Saeed.

"There are six people at the house, a woman and five men?" A single finger came up.

"Good. That's the idea. How easy life would be if we all co-operated," Saeed continued.

"There are two guards on duty at any one time, one inside and one outside?" Again a single finger came up and Khalaf started to pour the water in. Realizing it had been a trick the man violently shook his hands.

"Oh, I'm sorry my friend, did you make a mistake about that answer?" Saeed asked in an oily smooth voice, loaded with menace. One finger rose.

"Stop!! Khalaf, I think he made a genuine mistake," said Saeed in the same oily voice. The session went on for an hour, but to the victim it seemed like a lifetime.

Baum entered the room and vomited at the sight which met his eyes. "What the hell is going on?" I don't like these bastards, but you can't do this," he complained wiping his mouth with the back of his hand.

"I can do what I want. If you have a problem with that, take it up with your senior officer. Now get out and stay out," ordered Saeed, annoyed at the interruption.

Baum left. Then there was the sound of him retching again from outside the door.

"Sorry for that interruption. Where were we? Ah yes, I think we have about done my friend. You have been a good boy, so Yousef will not hurt you anymore," promised Saeed.

It took some time for them to get the man out of the contraption. On release, the pain was worse than ever, as fire coursed through his groin, but it started to ease as his bladder emptied.

"As I said to your friend, we will hold you for a few days and after we have our friends back, we will let you go. Let this be a lesson to you, don't take people hostages when you don't know who they are," Saeed chided.

"I hope Ali and Masood will be alright. This waiting with no news is getting to me," moaned Mel.

"Yes doll, it's not doing me any good either, but Saeed did say he would contact us as soon as he had anything to tell us. I think I believe him," assured Cindy.

Bring, bring. The phone rang and made them both jump. Cindy answered it.

"Yes," she barked. Her nerves were as frayed as Mel's.

"Saeed here," said the oily voice. He made her skin crawl. She would have a word with Masood about him when he got back.

"I have some news on Masood and Ali," said Saeed.

"What? Where are they? Are they safe? Can we see them?" she stammered.

"Steady, Cindy. Steady. We know where they are and we are watching the place. We have caught two members of the gang and have questioned them and they have told us a lot, but we still have to rescue them. It will be tricky," said Saeed.

"What is he saying, Cindy?" begged Mel.

"Pick up the other phone and listen you daft cow," snapped Cindy, trying to listen to Saeed.

"Pardon Cindy, I do not understand," Saeed said.

"No. Not you. I was talking to Mel about the other phone," apologized Cindy.

"Ah," said Saeed. "Then I will continue. We will be mounting a rescue very early in the morning tomorrow. They are due to go to the bank in the morning to collect the ransom, and they will be celebrating tonight, thinking it has all gone their way."

"How do you know all this?" demanded Cindy.

"As I told you, we captured two of the gang and they were very helpful," assured Saeed.

"But I thought these people were supposed to be nasty bastards," she said.

"They are Cindy, believe me. But I have even nastier bastards working for me," replied Saeed, in a tone which made her blood run cold.

"Is there anything we can do to help?" asked Mel from the other phone.

"No. Not at the moment. I will let you know when it is all over. Even after we rescue them, it may be a little time before you can see Masood or Ali. They will have to talk to the police, you understand," said Saeed. He had no intention of doing all this work for nothing.

CHAPTER TWENTY SEVEN
Death or Glory for Someone

He and his men spent the rest of the afternoon and night going over their plan and making sure they all knew exactly what was being done, and by who. They all knew there would be no margin for error. Omar and Riad had been out in the forest around the house, and had spent the afternoon finding and clearing two routes through the dense forest to the hedge surrounding the house. They had also spent time watching the guard's pattern, to make sure it tied in with what they had been told by their captives.

"So you all understand. Khalaf, you will take out the guard as he comes down the north side of the house, at exactly this spot, which is the only place where the two guards are out of sight of each other, and anyone in the house. Asif, you will take out the other guard at this spot. Mayoub, you must be by the front door ready to open it as soon as the guards are killed," said Saeed.

"Yes, Saeed," they all nodded agreement.

"Omar, on the door being opened, you will have fifteen seconds to find the inside guard and deal with him before the alarm goes off. Yousef, Riad and I will go to the cellar door where Masood and Ali are, to make sure no one gets to them. Meanwhile, the rest of you take out all the other occupants," continued Saeed, "now, any questions?" They all shook their heads. They were professionals and knew just what to do.

They went to the dormitory room where they tried to get some sleep, but for most it was useless. Each of them had his own task to do, and each knew that maybe millions of lives in the future depended on them being successful. It was a restless time for all except, Omar. He was used to great pressure and had no doubt that he would be successful in his part.

Before leaving, Saeed paid a visit to the woman prisoner.

"I am sorry we had to get the information the way we did," he apologized.

"We would have done the same," she replied.

"Yes, but Yousef enjoys himself too much," said Saeed. "And it is never nice to torture a woman. We are going on our mission now and it occurred to me, you may wish to be with your friend," asked Saeed.

"Yes," she said eagerly, following him out of her room. He opened the door of the man's room and the stench of urine hit her like a wall. She gagged at first, which was understandable. The man had a lot to get rid of, and they were not going to take a chance on letting him go to the toilet and escaping, before they could affect a rescue.

"I have brought your friend," Saeed said as he opened the door. "And I wish to thank you both for the information you have provided. I had thought I would release you in a few days time but, as you can do us no further harm, I have decided I will release you now...." They looked at each other, confused. Phht Phht. The gun in Saeed's hand spat twice and they died still looking confused. "...at least... from this world," he finished the sentence, whilst closing the door.

It was 2:00am, when they left for the house. By 4:00am, they were all in position and ready to go. The guard walking casually on the north side of the house was dead before he even knew Khalaf had got him. He had followed the cleared path to the hedge, made that afternoon by Riad and Omar. The giant stood as still as a statue until the guard was level with him on the other side of the hedge. Then Khalaf's huge hand reached through the hedge and closed on the man's throat, crushing his windpipe and any sound the guard could have made. Khalaf dragged him through the thick hedge breaking his neck on the way through, and then threw the lifeless body to the ground. Job done, he took the dead man's weapons and, in an incredible bound, was over the hedge.

The guard on the south side had as little chance as his friend. He was walking along lighting a cigarette, when Asif rose out of the ground. The look of surprise was still on his face as his severed head hit the ground. Asif was showered in blood, but that did not matter. He wanted it that way. It would help to make the others hesitate when they saw him and that gave him an edge. A split second edge was all he needed. The long knife he had used was special to him. Its blade was made from the finest Toledo steel and honed to unimaginable sharpness. It had been a present from a Saudi Prince who Asif had helped, on more than one occasion, to remove embarrassing gossips.

Mayoub was kneeling by the front door within seconds of this happening, and had the lock picked in a flash. He tested the door to ensure it had no bolt behind it, and it gave, ready to open. Omar was ready and as Mayoub pushed the door, he slid inside. It was pitch black, and his heart was pounding loudly enough to wake the house, not from fear, but excitement. This moment was what he lived for. His stealth and cunning against his enemy was everything to him. It was the greatest buzz of all, and to add to it he was also up against the clock. If the alarm went off before he found and killed his prey, then all could be lost.

Omar had prepared for this type of moment so many times before and his eyes recovered from going into a darkened room much quicker than most. He had trained them to do so. The hall was empty and he moved to the room on the left. The door was open and the room was empty. He heard a noise at the rear of the house and went to the end of the hall. There was a crack of light coming from the kitchen. It seemed like hours since he came through the front door, but it was only a few seconds. Looking through the crack of the open door, he saw the guard coming towards the door with a steaming mug in his hand. This would be too easy. What kind of terrorists were these? They had no pride in their work!

As the door opened, Omar struck. His left, gloved fist rammed full into the guard's mouth stifling any noise. His right hand, driving the long-bladed stiletto up at an angle through the man's jaw and into his brain. A few deft flicks of Omar's wrist scrambled the guard's brain. Omar lowered him to the floor, just as the alarm went off. The noise was deafening and instinctively he covered his ears for a moment.

"What was that?" asked Ali who had always had keen hearing.

"I didn't hear anything," answered Masood.

"Shsh," Ali was at the door listening. I am sure I just heard a crash.

"Probably one of them dropped a cup or something," said a sleepy Masood.

"What, at this time of the morning?" asked Ali.

"Well, we know at least one of them is on patrol in the house. Now let me get some sleep, as I am going to the bank later and I will need to be alert for a chance to escape," moaned Masood.

"Perhaps we are being rescued," said Ali full of hope.

"I told you I didn't hear anything. Now shut up and stop wishful thinking. Those bastards who have been watching us this past month were not as good as I thought," complained Masood.

They both heard the key turn in the lock, and they froze. Then the alarm went off, and all hell broke loose. Saeed came through the now unlocked door just as the alarm went off. His whispered warning to Masood and Ali coincided with the start of the alarm. Then they heard the sound of heavy footfalls on the stairs as the rest of the kidnappers came rushing down, guns in hand, heading for the room they were in. Hans was in front and seeing a shadowy figure near the front door, he fired on the run. Crack! But his shot was well wide of the mark. Riad had no such problem. Crack! Spoke the automatic in his hand. Hans was dead when his right foot hit the bottom step of the stairs. He fell headlong into the wall facing the stairs, and crumpled into a heap on the floor.

Herman, the leader, was right behind Hans and tripped over his body as he reached the bottom of the stairs. Tripping over Hans' prone body saved him for now, as Mayoub's bullet winged over his head. Picking himself up, he headed for Masood and Ali's prison room. Even if he died in the end, he was going to kill them as he had promised. He ran straight into the fist of Khalaf and went down like a pole-axed bear, leaving Helga alone. She was mid-stride, halfway down the stairs, when the lights came on and she saw Yousef and Riad guarding the door she wanted to go through. She made the bottom step with a jump taking them all by surprise, turned and with two shots killed Yousef and Riad. They slumped to either side of the doorway, as if to indicate to her she should go through, which she tried to do. Crack! Crack! Saeed's shots shattered her shoulders as she came through the door and she spun backwards onto the floor of the hall. From her position on the floor, Khalaf looked even taller than he was. Her gun was still in her hand and although she could do nothing with it, he placed his huge foot on her hand and ground it into the floorboards.

"Arrrrgh. Do your worst, you bastard," Helga spat through a sea of pain.

He just grinned, bent down, and grabbed her by the hair, dragging her to her feet. Her gun fell from her now, crushed hand, and clattered on the floor.

"We are saved, Masood. We are saved," shouted Ali, throwing his still bound arms over Masood and hugging him hard. "Thank you, thank you whoever you are," he shouted at Saeed. Letting go of Masood, he proffered his hands for the ropes to be cut.

"I think we will leave them on for the time being," said Saeed. "We have some questions for you. You may be more co-operative, if they are left where they are."

"But, I thought you were here to rescue us," asked Ali.

"We are. But all in good time eh," replied Saeed.

Ali looked at Masood in utter disbelief. His moment of joy had turned to confusion and he was like a lost little boy.

Herman was coming around and Saeed wanted to talk to him.

"So Herman, your plan has come to nothing. Do you want to tell me what else was supposed to happen today?" asked Saeed, whilst his captive glared defiantly at him. "Lost your tongue, eh? Well, let me tell you what was supposed to happen. You were taking Masood to the bank today to collect ten million Deutsche marks and it will still be there waiting for you."

"How do you know this?" growled Herman, confused.

"I know a lot. Your visitors of the other day were very helpful when we stopped them for a chat," explained Saeed gloating.

"They would not have told you," challenged a defiant Herman.

Saeed looked down at the body of Yousef.

"They did, thanks to that man," said Saeed, pointing at the body of Yousef. "You could say his performance on them was his finest hour."

"What do you intend to do with us now, pig?" spat Helga, in great pain from her shattered shoulders. "Give us to the police?"

"Oh no, nothing that grand," said Saeed. "I understand you do nasty things to your captives," Saeed challenged. "So I have something very special in mind for you. You have made me very unhappy the last few days, and you must pay for that."

It was dawn when Herman had finished carrying his dead comrades over to a spot Saeed had chosen in the corner of the garden.

"Now dig," ordered Saeed.

"What for?" challenged Herman.

"We are going to bury your friends. It's the least a true soldier can do," answered Saeed.

Herman dug steadily in the soft soil for four hours.

"It is big enough," protested Herman.

"Yes it is," answered Khalaf, hitting Herman on the back of the head. He fell to his knees, and Khalaf held him while others bound him hand and foot. This done, they threw him in the hole he had dug. Helga was dragged over tied and screaming, and shoved in the hole next to Herman.

"Stop," shouted Ali. "I don't know what you intend to do to her, but I have some payback of my own if you will cut me free."

Intrigued by this sudden outburst, Saeed cut Ali free.

"Be my guest Ali, she is no doubt a nasty cow anyway," laughed Saeed.

Ali jumped down into the pit landing on Helga, the pain from her shattered shoulders making her scream.

"Remember me bitch," Ali asked rhetorically. "I told you one day I would cut your black heart out and you laughed. Not so funny now eh, bitch." Sphht. Helga spat at Ali, but he was expecting it and moved his head out of the way.

"Do your worst you pig," she challenged. The group looked down into the hole fascinated as Ali grabbed her blouse and ripped it apart along with the bra she was wearing.

"Knife," Ali demanded to a surprised Omar, who handed him his without question.

"What are you going to do, Ali," shouted Masood.

"Her breasts are too large," Ali replied coldly. "I'm going to reduce them a bit," answered Ali running his thumb down the blade of the knife and drawing blood.

Helga was now sweating profusely and her defiant look had been replaced by a look of terror.

"You cannot let him do this, it is barbaric," she shouted at the assembled group.

"You killed our friends, Yousef and Riad, bitch," sneered Khalaf. "You expect us to stop him after that," he laughed.

Ali was smiling down at her now and brushing the blade across her bare breasts. She broke as all bullies do.

"Please," she begged. Sweat pouring from her exposed body. "You cannot do this." She was terrified now, tears streaming from her bulging eyes and her lips trembling with every word, and Ali was enjoying every second, he flicked the razor sharp knife across her breasts and the word Ali oozed in blood from her skin.

"I knew you were gutless you bitch," he said rising from his position on her stomach and returning the knife to a dumbstruck Omar.

"Thank you," was all Ali said, as Khalaf helped him from the hole.

"Bastard," Helga shouted after him while to her horror, Khalaf and the others threw the dead terrorists in alongside, and on top of them, and started to fill the hole in.

"You lying bastard," Herman shouted.

"Me?" questioned Saeed, grinning. "All I said, was I had something very special in mind for you."

They were still screaming as the soft earth started to cover them. It was some time before the earth stopped moving, and their screaming ceased.

"Do you have a fate like that in mind for us?" asked Masood.

"Not at all, my friend," answered Saeed. "You are far more important than that scum."

"So what do you intend to do with us?" asked Masood.

"Well first, we are going to the bank as there is the little matter of some money you have arranged to draw out. We thought we would come along and help you carry it," suggested a smiling Saeed.

Masood did not ask any more questions. He was fascinated by Saeed and what he may have in mind.

CHAPTER TWENTY EIGHT
Coming into Money

"I'm worried Masood," confessed Ali, as they got into the car to go to the bank.

"Why? They will not harm us, they need us," assured Masood.

"So why are we going to the bank?" asked a confused Ali.

"I don't know my friend, but worrying about it won't help. Let's just wait and see what happens," said Masood.

After burying Helga, Herman, and the others, Saeed telephoned Abdul Aziz. After all, who was going to complain about him making a long distance telephone call? The bill payers had gone underground for good, so to speak.

"The rescue was a success, Abdul," Saeed boasted.

"Good, did we take any casualties?" asked Abdul.

"Yes, I am afraid we lost two, Riad and Yousef. I have arranged for the local police to collect their bodies for now. Would you make arrangements for them to be flown home? They played their part well and were brave men, who we could not have done without," said Saeed.

"I will do all that. What of Jaleel and Beg? Where are they now?" asked Abdul.

They are here with us. I propose to send them back to Monte Carlo, in the hope that we are not too late to get the information on the next bomb, continued Saeed."

"I agree it is the best thing to do. I would like to bring them here, and get some answers from them, but I think we have to let matters unfold for some time to come," Abdul instructed.

"I will take care of that today and they will be back in their hotel by tonight," confirmed Saeed.

"I am just glad that we had no interference from the Libyans," said Abdul.

"No, and you won't. They interfered with Mel and Cindy while they were in London and have been dealt with," answered Saeed.

"Thank God for that," said Abdul, putting the phone down.

Saeed ended the call and ordered everyone to gather at the cars.

They travelled to the bank in silence. On arrival, the two identical Mercedes parked one behind the other. Ali stayed in one of the cars with Asif and Mayoub. Masood, Saeed, Khalaf and Omar went into the bank.

"Good afternoon, Mr Jaleel. A pleasure to see you again," said the cashier. "I will just get the manager for you." The manager had already seen them come into the bank, and was holding his office door open and beckoning them in.

"Good afternoon, Mr Jaleel. I have your money ready and I see you have brought your own security. Do you wish to use my office to count it?" asked the manager.

"That will not be necessary…," replied Masood. "…after all, if I can't trust my own bank, who can I trust!" he laughed. The money was inside two security boxes, and the manager lifted the lids, just to show them they were full.

"We have taken the liberty of making the amount up in as large denomination notes as possible. Is that alright?" inquired the manager.

"That will be fine, thank you," replied Masood.

"If you would just sign here," asked the manager, indicating the line for Masood.

They were in and out of the bank in ten minutes, with Khalaf carrying one box, and Saeed and Omar the other. Once back in the car, Masood could contain his curiosity no longer.

"So what happens now, Saeed?" asked Masood.

"We will take you to the airport where a private jet is waiting to take you back to Monte Carlo for a reunion with Cindy and Mel," said Saeed.

"And that's it?" asked Masood. "No torture."

"Yes! At least for now," said Saeed. "There may come a time in the future when we will need to talk, but for now we have done our duty. Some have paid a heavy price to release you, but we knew that before we went into the house," said Saeed thoughtfully.

"So what happens to my money?" asked Masood.

"Oh that! Just look on that as your way of saying thank you to us for saving your miserable lives, and be grateful you're not in that hole with Helga and her boss. We will look on it as a retirement fund for the future, eh Khalaf." Saeed roared with laughter and Khalaf was laughing so hard he nearly crashed the car.

"I can live with that," said Masood. "What about you Ali?"

"No problem," said a relieved Ali.

They stopped off at the police station to thank Baum for his help and inform him there was some clearing up to do at the house. It will remain a mystery to this day whether Saeed forgot to tell Baum about Helga and the leader's whereabouts deliberately, or if it just slipped his mind.

CHAPTER TWENTY NINE
Hugs Worth More than Money Can Buy

"I'm so relieved to be going back to Monte Carlo," said Ali.

"Yes. Even I thought we had had it that time. Cindy and Mel are in for a surprise," said a happy Masood.

"How can we surprise them? Saeed is bound to have told them we are coming," said Ali. "And look at the state of us. I need a bath after our time in that stinking room, and my clothes are filthy."

He was right he looked a mess. His black trousers looked grey and brown with dust and earth. His shirt was spattered with blood from the wounds in Helgas's shoulders when he landed on her in the grave. Masood was slightly tidier, but still a mess and they both needed a shave and bath.

"No, Ali. Ten million does, at least, buy us some silence," smiled Masood.

"Great. I can't wait to see their faces," laughed Ali.

"Yes. I called the hotel while we were in the bank and told Bernard to prepare a feast, but to make sure Cindy and Mel don't find out," laughed Masood again.

The Rolls Royce limo was waiting when they landed, and they were whisked to the hotel service entrance where they entered by the kitchen door. Bernard had sent out for new clothes for them and they were waiting in the rooms which had been prepared for them to bathe and change in. An hour after arriving at the hotel, they were ready to meet the girls.

Knock, knock.

Cindy and Mel were so nervous that they jumped at the unexpected noise.

"Oh God, Mel! Answer it will you? I can't face anyone," said Cindy. She was expecting bad news and this was it.

"Yes," shouted Mel through the door. "What do you want?"

"Room service, Mademoiselle," was the reply.

"Go away! We haven't ordered anything," Mel shouted back.

"Please. It is from the manager, and I will lose my job if I take it back," the voice pleaded.

"Right," said Mel wrenching the door open. She was determined to get rid of this nuisance.

Cindy was also heading for the door, which was lucky, as she was there to catch Mel as she fainted backwards through the open door. The force of Mel's fall knocked Cindy to the floor as well.

"What a fine way to welcome us home," boomed a smiling Masood. Ali was by now, holding Mel, while Cindy was getting up.

"You! You bastard, you rotten bastard!" Cindy shouted at Masood. He was now holding her and squeezing her so tightly she could say no more. It did not stop her from beating her clenched fists on his back though.

"Why didn't you tell us you were safe?" Cindy demanded. When he let her go, she slapped him across the face. He just smiled. This was his Cindy, and he knew he would pay for his joke later.

Mel was coming around now. Ali was still holding her and was running his hands through her hair.

"Wh, why did you not call us to tell us you were coming?" Mel demanded.

"Shsh my love," said Ali. "It is not important. We are here now and I will never leave you again."

The girls had not eaten since they arrived back in Monte Carlo. Ali and Masood were also very hungry. The feast Bernard had arranged arrived and was devoured at record speed, washed down with lots of champagne. At the end of the meal, they retired to their bedrooms, and to each other. They were all too exhausted to make love, but that would come another day. Only, Cindy was awake when Ali entered Masood's bedroom during the early hours.

She watched in silent fascination as he repeated the name of a town, some numbers and a series of letters. He did this three times, and always the same information, in the same order and then he left.

In the morning, she asked Ali what he was doing in their bedroom the night before.

"I don't know what you're talking about," he denied. "I never left Mel all night."

She realized as he continued to protest, that he really believed what he was saying, and that he must have been sleep-walking.

CHAPTER THIRTY
Tears and Recriminations

"We have some questions for you two bastards," announced Cindy at breakfast.

"Why?" asked a sleepy-eyed Ali. "What have we done?"

"That's exactly what we want to know. You're mixed up in something nasty. We have been kidnapped and beaten by men we have never met before. We have a right to know what the hell is going on," demanded an angry Cindy.

"What do you mean kidnapped and beaten?" asked Masood, very confused.

Cindy and Mel both suddenly realized that in all the excitement of them coming back last evening, the incident in London had not even been mentioned. Cindy pulled back her lips to reveal her missing tooth.

"We were grabbed by two men while we were shopping on Bond Street, then taken to a warehouse, and tied up," said Cindy.

Mel was starting to cry. Ali went to hold her, but she pushed him away. The memories of what happened were overcoming her feeling for him for now.

"Who were these men?" demanded Masood.

"How the hell do we know?" snapped Cindy, remembering her beating, and the fight for her life.

"What did they want?" pleaded Ali.

"For some reason, they wanted to know what we knew. We couldn't tell them anything because we didn't know anything," replied Mel, through the tears. Her crying, and the fact she would not let him near her was breaking Ali's heart.

"Did they hurt you?" asked Masood.

"Did they hurt us!" snarled Cindy, grabbing some tissues from a box on the table and scrubbing her makeup off. "What the fuck do you call this?"

Masood and Ali were shocked at the bruises on her face and neck.

"And these," snapped Mel, rising from her chair and ripping her dress off. Her legs and body were covered in yellowing bruises mostly finger-size.

"What bastard did this? I'll kill him!" screeched a distraught Ali.

"Too late," snapped Cindy. "Done that."

"What do you mean? Done that," demanded Masood.

"I mean, I killed the filthy bastard," shouted Cindy collapsing into a fit of sobbing.

"I, I, I don't understand," pleaded Ali. "What are you saying? If Saeed's men did this, I will kill them all."

"No! Not them. You stupid swine," snapped Mel. "If they had not come along, we would be dead by now. I think the men who helped us said the other men were from Libya."

Masood was trying to comfort Cindy, but she kept shrugging him away.

"Don't touch me," Cindy snapped in between sobs. "Not yet anyway."

"I am so sorry my love; I never meant this to happen. Honestly," said a distraught Masood.

"I suppose the other men who helped us work for you?" demanded Mel.

"Not quite," Masood replied.

"Then who the hell do they work for, and why were we taken to an embassy after the fight?" demanded Mel.

"What fight? You keep talking about a fight," asked Masood.

"After we were kidnapped by the two men, they took us to a warehouse in the dockland area and tied us to chairs. Then they asked us questions about you," replied Mel.

"What questions?" asked Ali.

"Shut up! I'm trying to tell you," shouted Mel. "We were very frightened and didn't know what they wanted. Then I heard this funny noise and one of them fell backwards with a big knife stuck in his neck. He grabbed my hair as he fell and I ended up lying on top of him as he died. It was horrible."

Masood was running his hands through his hair, his mind racing with fear and worry.

"And then?" urged Ali.

"If you fucking interrupt me once more, I will kill you," snapped Mel choking back her tears so she could go on.

"Sorry, my love," apologized Ali.

"Then the two who we had seen before, appeared and they were going to kill the other man who kidnapped us. But Cindy said he was a coward, and that he was good at hitting women who were tied up, but wouldn't fight her if she was free," continued Mel. She paused for a drink and also wiped her eyes. "One of the men gave Cindy a knife, and she fought the other man."

"And you killed him?" gasped Masood, looking at Cindy who was sobbing her heart out.

"Yes," Cindy whispered.

"I am so sorry, my love. This was never meant to happen. We would never put you in danger. I would cut my own throat before allowing you to be hurt," said Masood. He held her now, and she did not resist, as she sobbed away the pain and upset of the last few days.

"Ali," was all Mel said as she headed for the door. He followed her, glad to leave Masood and Cindy to their sorrow.

Once in their bedroom, Ali turned to Mel and tried to speak, but the words would not come. He was overwrought with guilt at placing the love of his life in such terrible danger.

"Sshh my darling," Mel said, placing a single finger gently on his trembling lips. "There will be time enough later, but for now just hold me tight."

He held her tight for a long time, until the crying had ceased, and she had fallen asleep.

They all slept fitfully for the rest of the day, and into the evening. It was Masood who woke up first. Even the events of the last forty-eight hours could not restrain his appetite for long.

It was a subdued meal for them, in their room, although Bernard and the staff begged them to attend a party in the hotel ballroom, to celebrate their safe return.

"It is a nice thought Bernard, but we are all very tired and we would not be good company," said Masood.

"As you wish Sir," said Bernard. I will cancel the party."

"No Bernard! Please, have the party anyway. It is just that Cindy and Mel have been very upset. You understand, they are not as strong as us men," explained Masood.

"Thank you. The staff will be most pleased," said Bernard hanging up the phone.

CHAPTER THIRTY ONE
Set Up for Life

"So Saeed, did you mean what you told Masood? Are we going to split the money, or what do you have in mind?" asked Khalaf.

"Of course I meant what I said. I think we have earned the money, but I propose that we give a share each to the family of Riad and Yousef," suggested Saeed.

"That is a good idea. They played their part well and earned their share," confirmed Khalaf, to nods of heads from all the others in the group.

"So, our share will come to over a million Deutsche marks each," said Omar. "Not bad for getting rid of some of the scum of the earth. I shall buy myself a boat with some of my share," he announced.

"What about our masters?" asked Asif.

"I have cleared it with everyone. They were all so pleased that we rescued Masood and Ali, as well as the good job you and Omar did in London. They are not only happy for us to keep the money, but I have a little surprise for you all," said Saeed grinning.

"And what is that? Don't keep us waiting," urged Khalaf.

"Our masters have matched the money from Masood, and we have double what you gentlemen thought," confirmed a smiling Saeed.

"Fantastic. I will retire," announced Khalaf.

"No, we cannot do that. It is the one condition which our masters imposed. We must stay on and complete our task, no matter how long that takes," said Saeed.

"But!" groaned Omar.

"There are no buts, Omar. It is the way they want it, and it will not be too long before you can go off and spend all your money on fast boats or slow horses," laughed Saeed, knowing Omar's weakness for women and gambling.

CHAPTER THIRTY TWO
Truthful Times

At breakfast the next morning, the girls were in better spirits, but in no mood to be lied too.

"So what is it to be, Masood? Ali? Are you going to tell us what is going on, or do we leave?" demanded a deadly earnest Cindy.

Ali was too stunned to speak.

"Go! Go where?" asked a confused Masood.

"Anywhere, away from you two, unless we get some answers," replied Cindy.

"Ask, and we will tell you," said Masood.

"Don't give us the run-around Masood. You know we don't know what to ask. I'm not even sure you know the whole thing, Masood," accused Cindy. She had a look like thunder on her face.

"I don't know what you mean," replied Masood.

"Ok," said Cindy and Mel together. They rose from their seats, and headed for the door.

"Wait! Wait! I don't know where to start," pleaded Masood.

"At the beginning, will do nicely," replied Mel, sarcastically.

Masood knew it was useless stalling any longer, "Before I explain, we must take a trip down to your boat, Mel," said Masood.

"Why?" asked Mel and Cindy.

"Trust me, we cannot talk here," Masood insisted.

They took the limo down to the boat and had a coffee at a marina-side café while the crew arrived.

"Where to, Mademoiselle?" asked the skipper.

"Just head out to sea, I will tell you when we are ready to return," Mel instructed.

They settled into the saloon and poured drinks for themselves, dismissing the steward to ensure privacy.

"Right Masood, why all the cloak and dagger stuff?" asked Cindy.

After taking a long drink from the whisky he had poured himself, he began. It took over an hour to explain all he could. The girls listened in riveted fascination and at the end of it, he slumped in his chair.

"My God!" said a surprised Mel, who had sat open- mouthed for the last half hour of Masood's explanation.

"You clever bastards!" joined in Cindy.

"You do not mind?" blurted out a surprised Ali.

"Mind! I've never heard anything like it in my life. It's like something out of a spy film, only we're living in it. No wonder money was no object. It makes what Cindy and I won look like petty cash," said Mel.

"And you Cindy, how do you feel about all this?" asked a bewildered Masood.

"Sounds about right to me," she replied grinning.

"What do you mean sounds about right?" asked a confused Masood.

"Well it all adds up now. You see a few nights ago, after you came back when you were rescued, I was half asleep when Ali came in our room," continued Cindy.

"What for?" asked Ali.

"I don't know, but you went over to Masood's side of the bed. Three times you repeated a name, some numbers and some letters," explained Cindy.

"What name?" asked Ali.

"I don't know. It was foreign sounding. Then you said the numbers and then some letters. You remember, I asked you the next morning why you came in our room and you said you didn't," continued Cindy.

"Yes, I remember that. But, I still don't remember coming into your room," said Ali even more baffled than before.

"Oh my God, Ali!" shouted Masood. "Now, it all makes sense. Do you remember about a week before Kutty died, he asked you to go and stay with him for a while."

"Yes," replied Ali, mystified.

"Well, it must have been while you were staying with him, that he placed all the information in your head," suggested Masood.

"He couldn't have. I would have remembered him doing that, wouldn't I?" asked Ali looking baffled.

"Not if he used a hypnotic technique called auto suggestion, thereby ensuring that even if questioned or tortured you could reveal nothing," explained Masood.

"Ugh! That's creepy," protested Ali. "So everything is in my head?"

"Yes Ali. It is you who has all the information they want, but even if you wanted to, you can only tell them when it is time to disarm a bomb and not before," said Masood, amazed at the genius of his friend Kutty.

"I don't know if I should be pleased or worried," said Ali.

"Well, at least it's out in the open now. Cindy and Mel can decide what they want to do in full knowledge of what is going on," said Masood.

"So, let me get this straight," said Cindy. "The men who are following you don't work for you at all?"

"I never said they did, my love," replied Masood.

"So, who the hell do they work for?" Cindy demanded.

"They are agents from all the countries we are blackmailing," said Masood.

"So when they rescued you, or us, why didn't they just torture any of us and find out what we know?" asked Cindy.

"I think the answer to that is they are playing a waiting game to let us make a mistake, and let them know how I get the information I pass on, about the town and code etc."

"So one day, they will get tired and capture you, and us, and that will be the end of that?" suggested Cindy.

"Yes, she has a point Masood, they won't stay away forever," chirped in Ali.

"A few days ago, I would have agreed with you both, but not anymore," replied Masood.

"Why what has changed?" asked Mel. "And another thing, is this the reason you were acting funny when we were in the airport at Dubai, Ali?

"Yes, I did not believe they would let us out of the country," Ali admitted.

CHAPTER THIRTY THREE
Revenge

"If the Libyans had not touched you my love, nothing would have changed. In kidnapping you, and hurting you, and worse still, making you fight that creature and kill him, they changed the rules. They must be taught a lesson," said Masood.

"No Masood!" said Ali. "What have you got in mind?"

"The Libyans must pay for what they did. It will, at the same time, serve as a lesson to the rest, that we are not to be harmed in any way in the future," said Masood thoughtfully.

"But…," started Ali.

"There are no buts," burst in Cindy."You did not have to fight for your life, or have to see what they did to me and Mel that day."

"Yes. You are right, it must be done. I had forgotten in all the events of the last few days," apologized Ali.

The boat was travelling at a steady twenty knots and the sea air was giving them all an appetite.

Mel rang for the steward and ordered sandwiches to be brought with champagne. Having brought it, the steward set it all out before leaving them again to private conversation.

"I will never forget what they did to me," growled Cindy.

"Nor me," sniffled Mel. "It was horrible."

"How shall we do it?" asked Ali.

"I'm not sure yet. Let me give it some thought while we eat," replied Masood.

They were just finishing their last sandwiches when Ali cried. "I have it."

"Then don't give it to me," said Mel lightening the moment.

"No, I have the solution," smiled Ali waving his arms about.

"Then tell us, Ali. Tell us," urged Cindy.

"It is simple. We wait for the next time there is a message about a town in Libya, and we tell them, as a demonstration, that we will not give them the code to disarm the bomb, but we will tell them the town. That way, they can evacuate the people and no one gets hurt, but we prove the point that we can hurt them anytime we want," smiled Ali proudly.

"Bravo Ali! Brilliant. Bloody brilliant," gushed Mel.

"That'll teach the bastards a lesson," chimed in Cindy.

"Well done my friend," smiled Masood, "Very appropriate."

Ali was too embarrassed to answer any of them and went as red as a beetroot.

Picking up the intercom, Mel asked the skipper to return to the marina.

As is often the case, they did not have long to wait. With the new found knowledge about Ali, they decided they did not have to travel and keep up with the pre-set itinerary of Kutty Krishnan. This had only been done to keep the followers guessing. So they decided to stay where they were, at least for now.

The next message was for a small town just outside Tripoli, in Libya, and could not have come at a better time. Masood made the call, but not to the contact for Libya. They had decided to make contact with Prince Faisal in Saudi Arabia.

"Good morning, Highness," greeted Masood, when the Prince finally answered.

"Good morning, Jaleel. What do you want and why have you called me?" growled Faisal, unhappy at being disturbed.

"You have our contact. Why do you not call him?" demanded Faisal.

"Because this is no ordinary call, and I felt you may want to listen to what I have to say. But if you're too busy, Highness…" said Masood.

Masood was putting the phone down when he heard the Prince shout.

"Wait!"

"Highness?" asked a grinning Masood, putting the phone on speaker so they could all hear what was said. "What is it?"

"As you are no doubt aware, my lady friend and her companion were recently attacked while in London," continued Masood.

"Yes yes," came the reply. "That was the Libyans and has nothing to do with me or my country."

"True, Highness. But I cannot allow this injury to my friends to go unpunished," said Masood. He had just a hint of threat in his voice.

"We saved your miserable skin in Germany, and theirs in London," argued Faisal. "You ungrateful dog."

"Name-calling will not help, Highness. If you are rude again, I will let the future take care of itself, and many will die," threatened Masood he looked up to find Ali, Mel, and Cindy all smiling at him.

Faisal was, by now, fuming, but he knew Masood had the whip hand and he had to control his notorious temper, at least for now.

"So what do you want, more money?" demanded Faisal.

"No, Highness. I am going to teach the Libyans a lesson, and you are going to help," said Masood.

Prince Faisal was so angry his hand was tearing a hole in the fine silk robe he was wearing; a beautiful creation made by a master craftsman in India It was hemmed in gold embroidery with an intricate pattern punctuated by Arabic verses from the Koran.

"How?" demanded Faisal, getting angrier by the second.

"Shut up and I will tell you," replied Masood. It was all he could do to stop himself from laughing out loud, as he knew Faisal would be red with temper at the other end of the phone, and ready to blow a gasket, but could say nothing to Masood, for fear he would cut the line.

"Go on," choked Faisal into the phone.

"I have the town and codes for the next device. It is in a small town near Tripoli. I will give you the name of the town, but not the codes or the frequency," said Masood calmly.

"But! But without those, the device will go off," shouted Faisal.

"Yes, Highness. In exactly three and three quarter hours time," continued Masood.

"But?" interrupted Faisal.

"Do not interrupt me again. You will need every minute, if lives are to be saved," urged Masood.

"Why are you doing this?" demanded Faisal.

"I told you. This is a message to Tripoli, and to you all. Next time any of us are hurt, I will not even give you the town name, then hundreds, or even thousands will die." Masood went on for a few more minutes, then repeated the town name and hung up.

It was a very worried Faisal who placed a personal call to Tripoli.

"They cannot do this," said the voice on the other end of the line.

"They can, and they have. We asked you not to interfere, but you went your own way, and this is where it gets you. I would start evacuation, if I were you," advised Faisal.

"But there are five thousand people in that town! Don't you know where the bomb is?"

"No, and you are wasting time while you are talking to me," said Faisal as he hung up.

The evacuation took three hours twenty five minutes, and was completed just in the nick of time. Then there was a loud boom, followed by a low rumble, and the town's telephone exchange turned into an expensive pile of rubble and wires.

Back at the hotel, Masood was eagerly waiting for the evening news. It came on as the third item.

"In Tripoli today, it has been announced that the cause of an explosion, which destroyed a telephone exchange in a nearby town, was due to a leaking gas main. Authorities say due to a vigilant police officer, there were only minor casualties."

"Yes!" shouted Masood, jumping out of his chair and punching the air. "That'll teach the bastards not to mess with us."

"Yippee!" shouted a delighted Ali, as he grabbed a bewildered Mel and danced her around the room. Cindy did not move. She had started to sob and the sobbing got louder.

"What is it my love?" asked a concerned Masood.

"I, I'm not sure I can ever forget those men, or what I had to do," Cindy managed to say before breaking out in uncontrollable sobbing.

"You were very brave," comforted Mel. "You saved my life and for that I will always be grateful. I am sure they would have killed us, had it not been for those two men and you Cindy. I am forever in your debt." Mel broke down as well, and the two girls left the room holding each other and sobbing.

"Will they ever forgive us?" asked a concerned Ali.

"I hope so, Ali. I hope so," was all Masood could say.

CHAPTER THIRTY FOUR
A Fresh Start for All

It was a lovely day when they awoke. The sun was bright and the birds were singing their best songs, as if to say, the past is over let's start anew.

"Breakfast everyone," announced Masood, knocking on Ali and Mel's door and entering without hesitation.

"Masood!" shouted Mel from under the bedclothes, leaving little to the imagination as to what she had been doing.

"Never speak with your mouth full Mel," joked Masood, turning and leaving as quickly as he had entered. It was a very embarrassed Mel that came to the breakfast table that morning.

"Morning, doll," smiled Cindy "Thought you'd already eaten," she laughed.

Smack! Was the sound as Mel slapped Masood across the face.

"Don't you ever come into our room when I'm eating, again," she laughed.

Now it was Masood's turn to change colour and he went bright red.

"Sorry Mel, honestly," he grinned. Ali, who was standing in the bedroom doorway, fell about laughing. He had never seen his friend embarrassed before.

"Serves you right," said Ali continuing laughing.

"Anyone got any ideas what to do today?" asked Masood, moving his jaw from side to side to make sure it wasn't broken.

"Yes," volunteered Mel. "My boat is ready. How about we go out for the day on it? We could take some food and have a picnic."

"Sounds like fun. After the last few days, we could all do with some of that," said Masood smiling.

"Now! Masood, we said we were making a fresh start and forgetting the past, so why bring it up again?" asked Cindy.

"Sorry, my love," he apologized. "You can punish me later."

"You should be so lucky," retorted Cindy.

"Bernard, please have the limo ready to take us to the marina in an hour, and make sure it has plenty of food and champagne in the boot," ordered Masood.

"Certainly, Mr Jaleel, will you be back today?" asked Bernard.

"We don't know. If we're staying out, I will let you know, just in case you think we have been kidnapped," laughed Masood grinning at Cindy.

"Masood!" the warning in Cindy's voice was unmistakable.

"Sorry, my love," he said, looking very sheepishly in her direction.

They were breakfasted and ready in an hour. The car was waiting.

"The Marina Alphonse," ordered Masood.

"Certainly, Sir," replied Alphonse.

"I have never seen the sea look so blue, or the flowers smell so sweet before," said Mel.

"No," agreed Cindy. "It's a wonderful day to make a new start in life."

There were many boats in the marina. They were of all shapes and sizes, but not many were larger than the Ali Cat.

"You renamed the boat," said a surprised and delighted Ali.

"Yes. I thought it was appropriate. Your name and I'm the cat that gets the cream," Mel laughed.

"Nice one, doll. Nice one," congratulated Cindy. It didn't take long for the crew and Alphonse to load the food and drink on board. They were soon nosing their way from the marina and out to sea.

"Fantastic boat, doll," said Cindy.

"Come and have a look downstairs," said Mel, leading the way down into the saloon, and passing two members of the crew. They had smart new uniforms of dark blue trousers, and cream-coloured polo shirts with dark-blue banding around the sleeves.

"Wow!" said Cindy taking in the ivory-coloured leather seating and the polished wood fittings. "I didn't take any notice the other day doll, I was to busy waiting for Masood's explanation. It must be a full-time job polishing all this wood and brass. My mum would have a fit if she saw this."

"Certainly is beautiful, Mel," said Masood.

"Wait until you see the bedrooms," Mel said excitedly, leading them through the saloon.

She had made some changes. Now, the first bedroom was a riot of white silk with roses embroidered all over it. Even the ceiling had a ruffled section of material above the king size bed. The bed itself was deep and soft enough for the lightest person to sink into.

"If you press this panel here..." Mel said, "...it uncovers all these switches and you can turn the lights up or down. The television and video are controlled from here as well."

"Does it bring you a drink in bed?" asked Masood.

"No, you have to call the crew to do that," replied Mel.

"Well, will it...," started Masood.

"Masood, don't you dare," smirked Cindy. "That's my job, and you better not get any ideas about anyone filling my boots."

"No, my love," Masood smiled.

The second bedroom was in plush pink, with a centre rose on the ceiling made from pink silk, and exquisitely designed to form a perfect flower.

"This is gorgeous," cooed Cindy. "Can Masood and I stay in this one? Oh please say yes?"

"Of course you can, if you like it," assured Mel.

"Like it! Like it! What's not to like? It's fantastic!" said Cindy. She was besotted, and went around the room touching and running her hands over the material and the wood.

"And like the first one, it has its own bathroom," said Mel.

Cindy did not hear her. She was too caught up in the elegance of the room.

"Just one more to show you," said Mel, leading a reluctant Cindy out into the passageway.

"The master suite," announced Mel proudly.

It was an understatement if ever there was one. The room took up the whole width of the front section of the boat. Gold was the prevailing colour, with the material shot with fine silver thread at regular intervals.

Above the huge circular bed, was a circular mirror with cleverly concealed lighting that made the mirror appear to glow from within.

"Truly fantastic," said Ali. His words were echoed by Masood and Cindy.

"Makes me feel ashamed to own our hotel," Masood joked.

"And as promised Ali, we now have a double shower," said Mel smiling.

"I think that's our hint to leave, don't you, Cindy?" said Masood.

"No, Masood. You must be hungry," Mel teased. "Let's have some lunch up on deck. The crew will have it ready by now."

"Just don't suggest a swim," joked Ali. "Or I'm off."

It was a hot day and the cruise speed of the boat gave a gentle breeze while they ate.

"Look, dolphins!" gasped Cindy rushing to the side of the boat. "Tell the driver not to hit them," she urged.

"He won't, and he is the Captain, not the driver," scolded Mel jokingly.

It was amazing to see the dolphins racing alongside the boat, playing and diving, in an endless game of chase. It was mid afternoon, when they went to their cabins for a rest, the exhaustion of recent events still upon them.

"This is an amazing boat, Masood. Would you like one like this?" asked Cindy.

"No, I'm not really a sailor, but I am buying a purpose-built plane," Masood boasted.

"Flash bastard," smiled Cindy.

"Did I tell you, Ali and I went to Stockholm, while you and Mel were in London?" asked Masood.

"No," said Cindy.

"Well we did, and I bought something a bit special for you," smiled Masood.

"Not more jewels?" asked Cindy.

"No, my love this," he said, reaching into a bag he had brought with him onto the boat, and pulling out the sand-encrusted whip. Her eyes glazed over as she looked at it, then he gave it her to hold. She ran it through her fingers.

"What's it covered in?" asked Cindy.

"Very, fine sand, they told me. Used properly, it just takes a single layer of skin off with each stroke," smiled Masood.

"Good, because you have some serious punishment coming for everything you've put us through over the last week, you swine," smiled Cindy flexing the whip. Her eyes were just slits now as he started to undress.

Masood shivered with anticipation, this could be a time to remember.

Cindy had her own ideas about that, and she was going to practise with the whip, until she was perfect. She meant what she said. Masood had some pain to go through for what had happened over the last few days. It was not going to be all pleasure.

"You have done wonders with this boat Mel," said Ali.

"Yes, I'm glad you like what has been done. Now, shall we test the bed or are you tired?" asked Mel.

"Not tired at all, but I do have something to tell you," confessed Ali.

"Is it bad Ali? If it is, I don't want to know. I have had enough to put up with recently," replied Mel.

"I'm not sure, but it is something that happened while you were away, and I feel guilty about it," continued Ali.

"Is it another woman?" asked Mel.

"In a way, yes, and in way, no. There was this stewardess on the flight to Hamburg," confided Ali.

"You and stewardesses? Did you screw her?" demanded Mel.

"No!"

"Then, what's the problem?" she demanded.

"Well, the man who was trying to sell Masood a plane brought her to an evening out while we were in Hamburg," went on Ali.

"And that's where you screwed her?" demanded Mel.

"No!" shouted Ali.

"Then, what are you on about?" Mel asked.

"During the evening, we danced, and we got hot, and went into the garden for some fresh air," Ali continued.

"And," she urged.

"She pulled him out and nearly swallowed him," confessed Ali.

"My God! She must have had a big mouth," Mel said, trying hard not to laugh at Ali's obvious discomfort. She could hold her laughter no more, and fell on the big bed, laughing so much the tears ran down her face.

"You're not angry?" asked Ali confused.

"Is she the one they buried alive?" Mel asked through tears of laughter.

"Yes."

"Then she is not around to tell anyone how big you are is she?" Ali was lying next to her now, and he looked ashamed and like a lost little boy.

"But I?"

"Did you want it to happen or not?" asked Mel more serious now.

"No. She tricked me, but I did cum in her," said Ali.

"Not surprised, if she had nearly all of him down her throat," laughed Mel, tears rolling down her cheeks again.

"I feel very ashamed I could not control myself," admitted Ali.

"Sshh Ali. You are mine, and we have a new life to start. I have an ache only you can kiss better."

She took his hand and led him from the huge bed.

"You can try to make it up to me in our new shower," she said pulling him inside.

The hiss of the powerful water jets drowned out the outside world as they got lost in the heat of the shower and their passion.

The End

Printed in the United Kingdom
by Lightning Source UK Ltd.
132118UK00002B/58-138/P

9 781934 925225